TEMPLAR

Paul Bannister

Paul Bannister has asserted his right under the Copyright, Design and Patents Act 1988, to be identified as the author of this work.

ISBN 978-1-911445-06-5

First published in 2016 by Endeavour Press Ltd.

Printed and bound in Great Britain by Clays Ltd, St Ives plc

Endeavour Press is the UK's leading independent publisher.

We publish a wide range of genres including history, crime, romance, historical fiction and thrillers.

Every week, we give away free e-books.

For more information about our titles, go to our website:
www.endeavourpress.com/our-books/

Or sign up for our newsletter at:
www.endeavourpress.com

Also available by Paul Bannister by Endeavour Press:

Crusader

Templar

As well as the bestselling Forgotten Emperor series set in Roman Britain.

Table of Contents

Introduction

Two voices are heard in this tale as Frederick de Banastre, baron and crusader, and his illegitimate son Alaric progress through the years after England's Magna Carta and recount events of the civil war and crusade which followed.

Theirs are varying viewpoints. One is a hardened pagan soldier, the other is inclined to the church although he too is a warrior.

Frederick fathered Alaric decades before but did not know it; the boy's mother gave him up to Frederick's sister to be brought up as her own son and entered the religious life. Only when Alaric was already a seasoned warrior in his own right did Frederick learn of his secret son, and father and son somehow united in their goal to bring a good king to England's throne.

'Templar' continues the narrative of two other books in the series, 'Crusader,' which details Frederick's life as a companion to the young Richard the Lionheart and of their adventures together as soldiers on the Third Crusade; and 'Treason' in which Frederick is an untrustworthy aide to Lionheart's brother and successor, King John.

When Lackland John lost his royal treasure, many thought it

was buried with the royal baggage train swamped in the tidal marshes of eastern England. In fact it was stolen by Frederick to use as leverage in a civil war between John and his northern barons.

'Templar' tells of the fate of that treasure; of Rome's cruel crusade to exterminate French heretics, and of the roles played by Frederick and his son Alaric in the bloody struggle for territory, gold and a throne.

Chapter I: Lackland
Alaric

If only we had known that King John would die so unexpectedly and so ingloriously, we would have handled matters differently. We could have averted a civil war, we might even have given ourselves a good monarch at last. But we acted too soon and we found ourselves with an aggressive French cuckoo firmly settled into our nest.

It was all a miserable set of misjudgements brought on by a grasping king, but the resentful barons also had a large role in it and so did the pirate named Eustace the Black Monk, and when all is done, war changes the landscape. That is what happened to us.

But, back to Lackland John, that cruel little creature from the hopelessly self-serving Plantagenet clan. His father, King Henry, had imprisoned his wife and deflowered his son's intended bride; all three princely brothers had fought their father and betrayed him and each other; and John had killed his nephew, the legitimate heir to the crown, with a clumsy castration. On the other hand, the nephew was no saint and had tried to kidnap his own grandmother.

But John was truly despicable. A serial lecher, he preyed

on his courtiers' wives and daughters, and greedily grabbed
their lands, jewels and gold. He also earned the wrath of
the pope and brought England under the double threat of a
papal-backed invasion and of going to hell and, not least, had
crippled the country with ruinous taxes to support his failed
military campaigns.

So you can see why we barons were less than sympathetic to
this Earl John, the third of old King Henry's sons to assume
the English crown, and unquestionably the runt of the royal
litter. Well, few could match glorious Richard the Lionheart,
Europe's leading warrior, or his elder brother Young King
Henry, who was as handsome and courageous as Lionheart
even if he was sadly empty-headed. It was John's misfortune to
be as small, dark and unprepossessing as his brothers were tall,
golden and dashing.

Looks were not the cause of our discontent. It was for the
crippling tax burdens he imposed on the earls and warlords
of England that we barons hated John so ferociously. He had
lost his possessions in France after squandering the tribute he
bled from us, and his army's defeat on the field of Bouvines
effectively rendered him impotent as a fighting king.

The earls of England saw their moment, brought the tyrant
to heel, and forced him to agree to reform. Should he fail to
keep his word, he would face a bloody insurrection that he
swore on his great seal would then be legal and justified. That

charter was made on a muddy little island in the Thames and it lasted about a week before John broke his vow. He repudiated the curbs placed on him, called up his allies from across the Channel, and went to war with his own earls.

He started at Rochester Castle, which had been captured by baronial forces. John undermined the outer wall and packed it with the fat of 40 swine to ignite a mine, which collapsed the southern corner of the keep. The garrison held out for two months, until they were starved out. John had them all, every knight and foot soldier, put to the sword. The tone of the war was set. Neither side would offer quarter to the other.

The news came to me from my father, Frederick de Banastre, Baron of Brotherton, Crusader and enemy of King John. "Alaric, matters are in a tangle," he told me grimly. "You know that a group of barons planned to offer the throne to the Earl of Leicester and that John and his spies thwarted us. Our noble king," he sneered, "scurried to the pope, who threatened us with excommunication and hellfire if we rebelled against our ordained and anointed ruler. Well, now there is another plot afoot. It's treason, but the great magnates of the north have asked Prince Louis, son of Philip of France, to take the English throne.

"They want to unseat John and install a foreigner. It's not a bad idea. It will bring peace with King Philip, and will rid us of the crippling taxations we've suffered to pay for the war with him. If John stays on the throne, he won't rest while his French possessions are lost, and he'll only tax us worse than ever as he struggles to get them back."

Prince Louis had acted on the barons' offer and in May 1216 landed unopposed in eastern Kent at the head of a sizeable army. The crossing was not without danger. John, licking his wounds after defeat in France, had a few months before called on the Norman knight Sir Hugh de Boves for support, offering him Norfolk and Suffolk as a reward, but the Narrow Sea between our island and France had been scene of a terrible tragedy.

On their short passage across the strait, a storm had swamped the fleet and 40,000 of Boves' followers, including women and children, were shipwrecked. Almost all drowned. Boves' corpse washed up near Yarmouth and chroniclers wrote that the beaches of south-east England were so thick with decomposing bodies that the very air stank.

Prince Louis wanted no repeat catastrophe, so employed as his naval commander a former Benedictine known as Eustace the Black Monk. The man had been the Count of Boulogne's seneschal before turning pirate, and had even been employed by King John to raid the coast of Normandy. He had changed allegiance after being outlawed by John for some additional, freelance plundering of English coastal villages.

Prince Louis employed the skilled seaman to deliver heavy

war engines to the English rebels, and sent a small advance force. It promptly occupied London while John was in the north, punishing the Scots for a rampage.

Eustace next took charge of a fleet of 600 ships and 80 cogs to carry the French invasion force to England, performing the task admirably despite heavy winds, and the French soon held much of south-east England. The Dauphin besieged Dover and his miners even brought down one of the gate towers, but the castle held.

"John's stretched thin," my father said. "He has the French and the barons to fight on the one hand, and the Scots on the other. But he has some allies, too. William Longsword has stayed loyal, as he should, he's John's half-brother." Frederick was speaking of the Earl of Salisbury, one of King Henry's bastards and a fearsome warrior and military commander. "There's also Pembroke, William Marshal, he's stayed loyal, too. They raised the siege at Lincoln. Significantly for us, Ranulf is also with them."

I nodded. Ranulf de Blondeville, sixth Earl of Chester, was our overlord. A magnate who held much of the midlands and northwest of England, Ranulf in the past had his differences with his king, and John, suspecting him of plotting with Welsh rebels, had stripped the earl of extensive estates and many of his castles, but had later reinstated them to keep his vassal's loyalty. To demonstrate his new trust, the king had even given

Ranulf licence to fortify other structures.

My father Frederick was one of Ranulf's barons, as one day I would be. As the only son, and a spurred knight, I would inherit not just our manor house, Bank Hall, but the spread of demesnes across Lancastershire that went with it. One day, I would be Baron Alaric de Banastre of Brotherton-on-Douglas, lord of Newton, Waleton, Munslow, Aston and Brotherton, master of a great stretch of the Fylde coast and its hinterland plain. All of it was territory which had been given to our ancestor Robert Banastre of Etaples by William the Bastard, Duke of Normandy and King of England, when he shared the spoils of a conqueror with his commanders and financiers.

I did not look forward to the duties of being baron. Four years before, I had lost to foul plague my beloved wife Virginia, who had given us two fine sons. Without her, the duties would be onerous and at age 38, I was ready to devote the rest of my earthly life to securing a place in the next world. I was considering entering the church, although I was a trained knight and seasoned campaigner.

My father was speaking again. Like me, he is a big man, a scarred and experienced Crusader who fought in France and the Holy Land with his friend and king, Richard of Aquitaine, whom men called Lionheart. Unlike most men, he has a strong sense of self. Frederick does not subsume his actions as being entirely for the glory of God. He pays his respects to the Lord but he takes responsibility for himself and maintains a clear-eyed view of the hypocrisy and manipulative nature of the clergy, while somehow remaining in good standing with the Church.

"Look here," he once said to me, "men spend 20 generations building cathedrals to glorify God, but we know the name of hardly a single one of the craftsmen, architects and stone masons who gave their lifetimes and skills to create these paeans in stone and glass. The men who acted as abbots and priors and treasurers are well-recorded, which implies that only matters relating to the church are important. And that, my boy, is horse dung."

Frederick's declaration was typical of his self-confidence. "Do you think God would begrudge the stonemasons and glassmakers their credit?" he asked. "He would not. They are the only ones in a thousand years to create stone buildings, but the snivelling priests who keep their proclamations wrapped in language inaccessible to the common people deny praise to any outsider. The clergy protect their own, and keep their secrets, they do not give credit to laymen. If you must become a friar to confirm your place in the next world, at least be aware of the hypocrisies."

I nodded, and said nothing of the pagan symbol, a small *mjollnir*, a Hammer of Thor talisman that he kept hung around his neck. Maybe that was why he was so unusually confident:

he had his feet in two religious camps. Certainly, when he spoke, people listened, but I felt that was because he saw things clearly, and not through some prism of religion or greed.

"Ranulf is a good man and is loyal now to England, but he still supports John, and it would be best for us all if John's man William Longsword were reined in," he rumbled. "However, we owe fealty to our earl. We have both put our hands between his and sworn sacred vows to serve him, and if we oppose Longsword we break those oaths." I nodded, remembering the time six years before when he and I had attended a secret convocation of northern barons.

Some famous warriors had been present: Crusaders like Jacquin de Grimshaw, whose skill with his great longsword Bonecrusher was matched only by his accuracy with an arbalest; Sir John Gardiner, a Templar whose cleverly-engineered siege tower had been the key that unlocked the walls of Acre; Berlage St Denys, a spiritual warrior-monk, and Sir Kelvin Barnstaple, a fighting man who had used his knowledge of castle-building to crack and slight strongholds across France and Palestine. Last but not least of our group was grizzled William FitzMorris, Lionheart's undefeated tourney captain, a man who had fought alongside his king in hundreds of victories both in battle and in tournaments.

These men and dozens more of their kind had gathered to

consider breaking their sacred oaths of fealty to John. All of us knew that we put our immortal souls in peril, but all of us were desperate. We had decided that the Frenchman Simon de Montfort, who was also Earl of Leicester, had the backing to be a powerful king. John got wind of the plot and it collapsed, perhaps for the best as I later found, for de Montfort was a cruel and harsh man.

After several more years that saw John humbled at Runnymede, some of the most powerful northern barons, including FitzWalter and de Vesci, whose wives had both been dishonoured by the king, made open rebellion and invited Louis of France to invade. First he sent a small advance force which arrived in London unhindered, then he followed with his invasion fleet.

Some royalist barons went over to the rebels' side. Astonishingly, they included William Longsword, John's half-brother, who had destroyed the French fleet at anchor in Flanders three years before. My father was stunned, but noted: "He must think John's cause is lost, but our seigneur Ranulf has stayed loyal to the king, as does Marshal, and he says he'll fight the French. At least Longsword no longer backs his brother the king. We do not openly commit to anyone, we don't want to fight with the northern barons against John and our own earl, who backs him. Nor do we wish to oppose our brothers of the north. We must sit quietly on the fence for now."

Things moved swiftly. In June, in the great cathedral of St Paul's, Louis was proclaimed King of England. He captured the capital, Winchester, and controlled almost half of England. John continued to fight him, and in October was travelling north to Newark when his baggage train was swamped in the tidal marshes of The Wash.

It was the day Frederick de Banastre seized a fortune. As Keeper of the Jewels, he closely monitored the royal regalia when it was being transported, and he had uncovered a scheme that John had secretly conceived. The king had agreed to pawn the crown jewels to the Jewish moneylender Isaac of Norwich, whom he was to meet at Newark, for John needed gold to hire Flemish mercenaries. Frederick was horrified. His duty was to guard the jewels and he knew that if the king sold them, it would be his, Frederick's, neck in the noose. But how could he stop the king?

The gods rolled the dice in my father's favour and matters could hardly have worked out better. Even before the disaster in the Wash changed everything, John had been stymied. He was taken ill after a greedy overindulgence in peaches and, forced to stay for a few days at the Bishop of Norwich's palace in Lynn until he was well enough to travel, had not been able to meet with Isaac. Instead, he commanded the moneylender to attend him a few days later.

The gods must have laughed among themselves, On the very first day of the resumed journey, the crossing of the tidal marshes turned into a disaster. John, soaked, chilled and panicked, relapsed into his illness and had to halt his journey again, this time at Swineshead Abbey. The Jew heard the news and arrived there but could not complete the agreement as the king was again too unwell to parley with him. It did not matter, the bargain could not have been struck. The jewels were not where John thought they were. My father and several companions had already taken possession of the choicest of England's crown regalia.

Frederick – I thought of him as Frederick, not Father, because I had grown up believing I was the son of another man - Frederick spirited away his loot with the help of friendly clergy, for John was no favourite of theirs. He took it to the Church of St Mary and the Holy Rood, in Donington, where a young monk called Walter of Pinchbeck was a friend of Frederick's tutor, Adam. He acted as the go-between and helped to persuade his abbot to cooperate. Frederick's intimidating presence, a gift of gold, antipathy towards John all played their part, and the regalia was hidden in a vault at the church.

John never knew he had been robbed. He died of dysentery at Newark on the Feast of St Luke, just a few weeks after the disaster at the Wash. "You can't imagine the relief I felt," Frederick grinned. "I was the king's Jewel Master. With John dead, I was the only person apart from my fellow conspirators who knew that the missing regalia wasn't under the quicksand and waters of the Wash. Isaac might have suspected something, but no Jew would go up against an English baron, so his silence was bought. It was a great relief to my unstretched neck that the king would never know what had happened."

After John's death, the question of succession was re-phrased and the barons largely withdrew their support of Prince Louis. Even Longsword rejoined the ranks of the royalists. Frederick explained it: "We could not lay our grievances about John at the feet of his son Henry of Winchester, the child was only nine years old. On the other hand, we were suspicious of old Marshal and much more so of devious Longsword, who had been a little too willing to turn his coat. They might act as regents and hand over the throne in seven or eight years' time, but on the other hand, they might try to assume it for themselves.

"We wanted a king, not a regent, but the boy Edward would not be able to control a country divided by civil war." Frederick scratched at a louse in his beard. "The new problem was Louis. He had an army on English soil, his nobles were arrogant and demanding; they wanted great parcels of our land in return for their military assistance, and we feared Louis would yield to them at our cost.

"We had to boot the French out of England. They even kept complaining about having to drink English beer, because we had no wine. Spoiled bastards."

Most of the barons had returned to the royalist camp when the news came of forces being raised to relieve Lincoln Castle, which was under siege by the French. I remember the day very well. It was a beautiful May morning in 1217 and Frederick and I were at Ranulf's palace at Chester, gone to speak with our lord about raising a levy.

Ranulf, who was not a tall man, looked up at us both. I may add that Frederick is a big, bearded, imposing man with the commanding air of the battle-hardened soldier he is. I may not have as much battle experience as he, although I have had a dozen years of campaigning in France, but I am even taller than my sire, and just as broad in the shoulders. I am a trained, spurred knight and only my confessor knows how shamefully many men I have killed.

"My duty is to prevent the northern earls from linking their forces to those of Louis," he said, almost without preamble. "As High Sheriff of Lancashire, Shropshire and Staffordshire, I can call on my vassals to raise a considerable force, and quickly." He eyed me warmly. I liked Ranulf and he had taken an interest in my education and training after my supposed father, also called Ranulf, had died.

"You both know, I suppose," he glanced at Frederick, "that last October Salisbury and Pembroke," – he meant the earls William Longsword and William Marshal – "acted swiftly at Gloucester when King John died." I did know that, it was a scandal.

As one of John's executors, our lord Ranulf de Blondeville had been expected to be a regent for the boy Edward Winchester but Marshal and Longsword had moved very swiftly. None of the executors were present when they convened a gathering of bishops and nobles and had William Marshal appointed regent. It was a coronation so hasty it was over before Ranulf even had word of it.

Only a handful of nobles and three bishops were in attendance, the Archbishop of Canterbury, who was supposed to crown England's king, was dancing attendance on Louis. They could not even use the real coronation regalia, for John had pawned some, and my father had spirited away the rest. It forced the officiants to make do with a simple gold band that was placed on the child's head by the Bishop of Gloucester.

Years later, a new pope announced that the coronation had not been properly carried out and ordered a second ceremony, which was conducted at Westminster.

Excluding the powerful Earl Ranulf from that first, hasty coronation could have led to more war, but the magnate graciously said he did not wish to assume the regent's role, and the threat of conflict vanished. Marshal wisely declared that the young king's intention was to rule by the precepts of Magna Carta and reissued the charter, which placated many and made them feel that Henry Winchester was a safer bet than Louis.

The passed-over regent, my liege Lord Ranulf de Blondeville, was no fool. He cleverly chose to combine his own interests with those of the nation and called on us and a fighting force to march against Saer de Quincy, the Earl of Winchester. De Quincy was Louis' man, but that was not Ranulf's chief reason for attacking him in his Leicestershire castle of Mountsorrel.

Ranulf was bitterly aware that De Quincy's ancestor had seized Mountsorrel from his great-grandfather, another Ranulf, and he wanted his ancient rights restored. We were going to fight the French, in England, to get the stronghold back.

Chapter II: Lincoln
Alaric

We arrived at Mountsorrel in a column of 4,800 men to stare up at the high granite walls which dominate the gently-flowing River Soar and to find the surrounding countryside had been stripped bare by the garrison De Quincy had installed inside his fortress.

I reined in Maximus, the splendid war-trained courser that was a gift from my father and looked at the array of banners fluttering from the battlements. We had halted a long bowshot from the walls and Earl Ranulf sighed. "It will have to be siege tactics," he said. He glanced around, sighted a copse of trees on a small hillock nearby and said: "We'll set ourselves up there."

Two days later, just as we were beginning to become comfortably established in our campaign tents, two mounted men cantered into camp. A quarter hour later, the summons came from Ranulf. "We're leaving for Lincoln," he said shortly. "The French have it besieged, and Marshal is heading there with the army. He's in Northampton at present. Even Willikin is on his way." He referred to William of Kensham, the leader of a number of bands of Kentish archers who were shredding the French invaders whenever they ventured out of their strongholds and went into the vast forest of the Weald.

Frederick asked Ranulf: "Who commands the forces inside Lincoln?" De Blondeville shrugged. "It's some mad bitch called Lady Nichola. She's always been a royalist, even in the days of John. I suppose he pupped her."

"Does she have enough to hold out against Louis' forces?"

"Don't know, we'll have to hurry, just in case."

So we force-marched 50 Roman miles across England in two days, following the fine Roman road of the Fosse Way, watching the mileposts count down the number of paces we still had to complete. We out-marched our baggage wagons and our heavy siege equipment; we watered our horses where we could in dew ponds on the dry wolds, crossed the Trent at Newark on a fine stone bridge that stands under the loom of its guardian castle, then headed on the arrow-straight road to where Lincoln stood proud on its steep mount.

We came close at dusk, and scouts rode back to tell us that the castelaine and her troops were holding out, so Ranulf halted us discreetly short of the campfires of the French besiegers while he sent messengers to communicate with William Marshal.

Soon enough, we were riding to a council of war, and the grizzled Earl laid out his plan. In the wolf light before true dawn, we would silently move up on the French rear-guard, circling and fording the River Witham to approach from the north and trap the besiegers against the water. The French had not built a palisade behind themselves, confident in their ability to capture the citadel quickly. Instead, they had merely established a semi-circular encampment of canvas and linen tents behind a ring of guard fires, using the river as their defensive wall on the south side of the city.

The earl's plan was for our archers – and we had battalions of them, reinforced by Willikins' Kentish bowmen – to loose a devastating storm of fire arrows which would fall steeply from high onto the flimsy tents of the sleepers. Under that rain of iron-tipped, goose-feathered and ash-shafted death, our heavy horsemen would race in to hack, trample and spear the panicked, drowsy enemy.

The Earl had other tricks up his embroidered linen sleeve. He positioned infantry in a half-circle of steel behind a deliberately-sited gap in our cavalry's squadrons. This would channel fugitives and trap all who fled through it. He also sent several thousand men to stay south of the river. They would drive back any fleeing French who attempted to cross to safety. A detachment of cavalry headed for the Roman bridge out of the city to seal that escape route, and Frederick and I were included in that task force.

The operation went just as planned. Hundreds of fire arrows coursed into the dark sky, path-finding an arc for 2,000 bowmen to follow. Each performed the same ritual as they loosed, then stooped for another clothyard-long ash, birch or poplar shaft that had been stabbed upright into the ground. Each archer nocked the shaft to the hempen bowstring, hauled it back almost to the ear, then loosed the missile. The rhythm was unvarying. Stoop, nock, bend, loose, stoop again, five, six arrows per minute to the constant thrumming of bowstrings and grunting of men's efforts as they bent their backs against the D-sectioned heartwood of the long yew bows.

The archers of Kent, Cheshire and Gwent out-shot any in the world, for Englishmen were encouraged to use the longbow and trained to it from boyhood. They did not draw with the strength of their arms alone, as did the French and others; the English and Welsh archers laid their whole body into the bow, using the big muscles of the back and shoulders to bend the horns of the weapon, generating enough force to lift a large man. It was a technique learned and practised over a decade or more, from childhood, with the stiffness of the bowstave matched to the boy's strength, and constantly increased as he grew.

In addition to the velocity of the arrows, which could kill through wrought-iron armour at a furlong's distance, or could cripple an unarmoured man at 350 yards, went the rapid fire of five or six shafts per minute. This withering rate frequently shot flat the enemy infantry whose normal protection was chain mail and leather. Archers made (and after battle would retrieve) their own marked arrowheads of beaten iron, shaping deadly needle bodkins to penetrate a knight's mail, or even his plate armour at short range. They created curved broadheads to slice through a soldier's Jack coat of leather and padding and barbed 'wolf' arrows to create fatal wounds in the more lightly-protected.

I knew and respected the firepower of a cohort of archers and felt a twinge of sympathy for the wretched French who were about to experience it as, under the whisper of the high-arcing arrows, we walked our coursers forward. My knees were almost touching the next man's on each side, we moved with cloth strips muting the jingle of bridle and bit, to the murmuration of riders shushing their mounts' soft whinnies.

The first fire arrows fell, causing small blazes that were lighting the encampment. Men, some of them impaled by arrows, were struggling out from under folds of burning canvas; brazen throated trumpets were calling to us, ordering the charge and we were cantering, now galloping in a thunder of hoofs and screaming the challenge of our war cries.

For myself, I was bellowing the old Crusader battle call: "Deus Vult!" and if God did indeed wish it, the French did not. To my right, I heard FitzMorris bawling like a bull, shouting his own favoured cry: "Dex Aie!" that requested God's help. Invisible behind my helm, I bared my teeth in a grin. FitzMorris didn't need any help in a skirmish, but his opponents certainly did.

Our horses' hoofs were thumping a shuddering tattoo and the familiar feelings washed over me. There is a terrible joy in racing into battle, a heart-pounding exhilaration in the charge, the fizzing thrill of danger, the animal exultation of hacking down at an enemy to spill his blood and break his bones. You are riding near-impregnable on a warhorse that is a trained battle machine, an irresistible, dangerous heavy beast that reacts just as you do, screaming, stamping and slashing, he with his yellow teeth and brutal iron-shod hoofs, you with longsword or mace or flail, all of them aimed at the heads and arms of the few who dare to stand up to your charge.

Maximus was trained to leap and kick at any who approached him from behind – it is a foot soldier's ploy to hamstring a war horse. My courser was also taught to bite and slash, and to respond to the pressure of my knees to turn, halt or accelerate, a method that left my hands free to wield weapons and shield. So we stabbed, slashed and battered our way through the tent lines, heading directly for the stone bridge that crossed the river.

From time to time, something struck me; once my left shoulder was numbed for a few moments by what I judged must have been a quarrel from an arbalest's crossbow, but the thudding gallop for the bridge was as every battle charge had become for me, an exercise in slowed time, a period when the moments go by so slowly you can coolly view what an opponent is doing, what his next moves will be, and you have aeons to counter them or strike a killing blow. It is as close as man can be to becoming a god himself, Christ forgive me, but there is exhilaration, pure feral joy in living as others are dying under your blood-streaked blade.

I arrived at the bridge against a storm of arrows, but most were broadhead missiles, which are much less lethal to an armoured knight than the needle-pointed bodkin heads. Those can pierce mail and make your day an unpleasant one, but the French are not noted archers, and the arrow storm that was clattering around us came from the Flemish mercenaries who had been ordered to clear us from the bridge.

Frederick was already there, hauling hard at the mouth of his big black destrier Sinner so he faced the missiles and would be better protected by his covering trapper, which I knew had reinforcements of leather in the padded gambeson that protected the horse's chest, ribs and neck. I was mildly surprised that he was riding Sinner, who was a very valuable tournament-trained beast, instead of using a much less expensive courser like my Maximus, but my time for musing was limited, and I wheeled alongside Baron Banastre and touched my helm with my armoured fist. "Nice day for it, Frederick," I said, my voice muffled behind my closed visor.

Frederick pushed his own visor upwards to afford a better view of events. "Here they come," he said with a timbre of satisfaction in his tone. "Let's get stuck into these upstarts from Paris." A straggling group of horsemen was moving towards us from the tent lines, many of the riders still buckling straps and tugging at mail coats, evidence of the surprise we had caused and the haste in which they had suited up in their armour. I saw one fellow with a design of blue and gold lilies on his surplice halt, swearing, so that a page who was running alongside his horse could scramble up to adjust his breastplate.

I glanced left and right. About four score of our knights were already on the bridge, waiting for the French assault. We would be difficult to dislodge from that narrow space. In the second row, the Templars Gardiner and Grimshaw were waiting, mounted knee to knee, chatting casually as if they were about to follow the hounds on a stag hunt. Grimshaw had discarded his favoured crossbow and was holding a heavy-bladed mace called a virge that is a brutal weapon. It is edged and flanged, and is used only by the strongest of men, who can chop through plate armour with it, something that sword or lance cannot do.

FitzMorris pushed through the ranks to come between Frederick and myself. "They don't look too eager," he said, nodding towards the mustering French. "And there's that whey-faced bastard traitor Caldor, with Louis' lot." Frederick grunted. "There's a lot of rebels who still want Louis as king, and I think many of them are facing us today." He squinted, for the sun was rising in the east and we were looking into it. "You know, they're still getting ready," he said. "Why do we wait for them, let's give them a thumping before they're set."

He pushed his horse forward and rode down the front rank to Earl Ranulf. I could only guess at the conversation, but the earl nodded and soon the word came down the line. "On my signal, charge them." The word went back through the files, the horses sensed the excitement and began restlessly passaging and stamping. Moments went by, then Ranulf gave a great shout, the drumbeats rolled their blood-stirring tempo and we were pouring off the bridge and forward, charging back the way we had come.

The French broke before we got to them. The front rank was sawing at their mounts' mouths and turning the beasts savagely away. I crashed into one chevalier in the third or fourth rank who was only half-turned, and he and his horse went down in a shuddering clatter. I had time to take a single, arm-jarring swipe at the side of his helmet and Maximus was rearing and striking out with his hoofs at the knight in front of me. He wore no helmet, so I could register that his eyes were wide, his mouth was an O of shock. He died that way as my swinging sword took him in the neck, half-severing his head from his shoulders.

The bloodspray of bright arterial gore jetted over my surplice, which carries the golden wheatsheaf of Chester on it, and most of the sheaf went from gold to crimson. I had no time to view the effect for the conflict was turning into a rout. I kicked Maximus in the ribs to urge him on. The next minutes were a blur of hacking at retreating backs, heads and shoulders. A northeastern baron I vaguely recognized knew me and fell to his knees in abject surrender. "I am Nicholas of Bedlington. I can pay ransom for my life." I leaned down and took his sword, waved over a foot soldier and instructed the fellow to find me with the captive after we had finished the business. Ransom could be lucrative.

On my right, I saw de Grimshaw unhorsed. His courser had taken a bolt through the neck and the poor beast sank to the ground, spilling the Templar. For a few moments his leg was trapped under the dying horse, and I hauled back on Maximus' rein to go to the knight's aid but he had already struggled to his feet and I eased. Then, seemingly from nowhere, a Norman rode him down and hacked at the unhorsed Templar, whose sword still lay on the ground. De Grimshaw batted at the blow with his gauntleted fist, which was covered in protective whalebone plates. It was enough to deflect the blade and send it skidding uselessly down his mailed left forearm. In one motion, he seized the Norman's boot in both hands and heaved hard to tip him off his horse.

The cavalryman hit the ground with a crash and Grimshaw was ducking under the horse's head to seize the dazed man. He grabbed the fellow's head two-handed and smashed it into his knee, then lifted and turned the unresisting body, crooked his armoured right forearm around the Frenchman's throat and grasped the chainmail that covered his own left bicep. The Templar's left hand went to the back of the man's helmet. Grimshaw was swift. He made a vicious upwards, heaving twist, sideways and back. There was a sharp cracking sound as the man's neck snapped. The Templar dropped the body, head lolling, scooped up his sword from the ground, coolly grabbed the bridle of the Norman's horse and heaved himself into the high-pommelled saddle. He glanced around, saw me and waved his sword. "Let's kill some more!" he called. And we both turned our mounts to rejoin the slaughter.

Meanwhile, Earl Marshal's deployments had worked well. A flood of those who tried to flee the field had run through the cavalry gap into the waiting spears of a shield wall and already were being disarmed and herded together.

A cohort of infantry had replaced our horsemen at the bridge, and Frenchmen and rebel barons – we captured 46 of those by day's end – were being rounded up even as the city gates were being opened to us.

Gardiner rode by me. "We have taken three earls," he hooted happily. "Three earls, Sir John?" I asked. "Well, two:

Winchester and Hereford," he said. "The third is Lincoln, who'd just been appointed by Louis, the upstart. Marshal says he'll give that earldom to your man Ranulf for his, well, for your help. Anyway, get inside the city, the earl says John's followers don't deserve clemency, the place can be sacked, so there's plunder to be had."

There was so much booty taken that the day was known as 'Lincoln Fair' by the men, who looted homes, emptied storehouses, and even sacked churches for their plate and hangings. The soldiers staggered away from Lincoln a day or two later, smoke-stained and bleary from drink and rape, carrying bolts of cloth, all imaginable household items from cooking pots to chickens, and with cartloads of looted food and drink. As for the French who escaped, the locals who had suffered in the war took revenge on those who tried to flee to London.

As the weary, dispirited fugitives passed through their towns, the inhabitants went after them with axes and clubs and a great many were slain. The villagers pelted them with dung but otherwise left unharmed the whores and camp-followers who were mostly English, but killed the retreating foot soldiers who were not. Few got back to the Tower. It was a huge disaster for Louis, who was clinging to London, and squandering forces on an unsuccessful siege of Dover Castle. Despairing, he sent to his father Philip for reinforcements.

Chapter III: Sandwich
Alaric

Defeat at Lincoln caused Louis to raise the siege of Dover, which had failed despite bribery, heavy siege equipment, and a successful mining operation that had led to the collapse of the gatehouse and capture of the barbican. Louis was havering, so he agreed to parlay with William Marshal, but the negotiations were fruitless.

Marshal told my father: "I met the slippery swine at Brentford and got him close to an end of hostilities, but the damn God-bothering bishops got in the way. Too many of them, including that traitor Canterbury, had gone over to Louis and it will evidently take a pardon from Rome for them to keep their possessions and that means weeks for a legate to go there, get the thing and come back.

"I almost got Louis to agree to a truce while the pardon was granted, but he heard that his father had persuaded his wife Blanche of Castile to send reinforcements and he backed away from our talks."

Frederick said that one thing came of Marshal's talks: he got to find out about the monk Eustace, who had once been John's man. "Another treacherous turncoat," Frederick growled.

"He was the count of Boulogne's bailiff and seneschal but stole from his master and was declared outlaw. He's a cunning fellow. He became a pirate and plagued English and French shipping in the straits, even was employed by both kings to prey on the other's vessels.

"Seems he held a castle in Guernsey and took the island of Sark, too, using them as bases for his raids on English coastal towns, including Folkestone. After Runnymede, he backed the rebel barons and of course Prince Louis, whose invasion forces and war engines he ferried across. Now, Marshal tells me that spies say Eustace is readying another fleet, to bring Philip's men to his son's aid, so the earl has set Hubert de Burgh to ready an English fleet to confound him. I said we'd be delighted to join in on that business."

Frederick paused and looked at me, "Hope you don't mind, this Eustace is a dangerous fellow and I know you're not a seaman. In fact, de Burgh nearly lost a skirmish off Dover last week, Eustace was all over the English ships until they bombarded the French with lime powder and blinded them. Then de Burgh's men were able to board and take a few ships in the melee. Eustace escaped, of course, so he'll be back, and likely with big numbers."

The prediction was accurate. In August, on St Bartholomew's Day, I found myself at the rail of the cog Stormbird, the ship of the Earl of Pembroke, William Marshal, who had stayed ashore at Sandwich by reason of his age. It was just one of the fleet of 40 ships from the Cinque Ports commanded by Philip d'Aubigny and the earl had attached me to the fighting men on board at my lord Chester's request. On the good saint's feast day, therefore, I found my unsailor-like self on a ship that was one of three patrolling to find the French. It was an enjoyable novelty to be afloat on this clear, bright summer's day while we moved slowly off the Kentish forefoot of England.

St Margaret's at Cliffe was to our west, its square church tower on the white chalk cliffs clearly visible in the early light. The sea was running fast, a cold green current ebbing out of the North Sea and into the Channel and we sailed slowly north towards the mouth of the estuary of the Thames.

Finally, we were off the small fishing village of Margate, under the chalk cliffs and the ruins of a stone signal tower built by the Romans. "This is the mouth of the Thames," the monk Adam of Lonsdale told me. I grasped the old cleric by his arm.

"You are a fount of knowledge," I told him, "but why you persist in coming on military expeditions, I have no idea. You should be on your knees in a priory, telling your prayers like a good beadsman." He smiled at me.

"Too many years of being a warrior," he explained. "You can't just leave an old warhorse in the stable. I'm quite prepared to go to God."

"Not this day," I said.

"Alaric, we do not know which day we'll be called," he told me gently. "Just be at peace with the idea."

Before I could respond, a bustle of activity caught our attention. A sailor was calling, pointing north-eastwards and the shipmaster was shouting orders involving the sails, so far as I could understand. I squinted in the direction the sailor was pointing and spotted several square shapes of white, then several more. The French were at sea.

It was a big fleet, we learned. There were about a dozen troopships headed by Eustace's flagship, the Great Ship of Bayonne, and 70 smaller vessels carrying supplies. We would later learn that 36 of the 125 knights in the fleet crowded the flagship, the rest were on three of the other larger vessels. Men at arms manned the remaining eight or so troopships, and every one of them was overloaded, most notably the flagship, which carried a huge siege catapult and some horses intended for Prince Louis.

As the size of the French fleet became obvious, I looked around at our trio, and comprehended at once why the sailing master had turned us back. What I did not know then was that our own flotilla of 16 large ships and 20 smaller vessels had waited in port until the invaders passed, and only then came out to follow them. We on Stormbird doubled back down the coast and with the brisk wind and the fast- flowing ebb tide soon came in sight of the English ships putting out into the Channel.

The French had the advantage of being to windward of us as well as the benefit of huge numbers, but our fleet commander De Burgh made one lunging feint of an attack, then quickly turned away to lure the enemy into breaking ranks. It worked. The French commander, Robert de Courtenay, ignored his admiral Eustace's advice not to follow and ordered his fleet to attack us.

I am still unsure of some of the events as I was feeling sea-queasy, and was unable to pay full attention, but De Burgh carried out some tacking manouevres I did not understand and we curled around the flank of the French and suddenly were upwind of them, and closing. Our archers took advantage of the brisk following breeze that allowed them extra range, and landed a steady hail of arrows on the troopships. By what I suppose was good seamanship, we kept the up-wind advantage for a considerable time and at quite a cost in wounded and dying invaders, before the French could effectively respond.

Our shipmaster was shouting new, urgent orders and we turned away from our harassment of a packed French troopship to hurry down the line to where the enemy flagship Bayonne had grappled the cog captained by Richard FitzJohn, who was one of King John's bastards. We were closest, and first there, so glided up to the side away from the battle, banged into the Bayonne and in seconds our mariners had grappling irons biting, hauled tight and lashed. I tapped the hilt of my sword Hwyl, which means 'spirit' or 'gusto' in the old Britonic language, taking comfort from the familiar feel of him.

A band of our boarders went swarming over the gunwales, I was swept up in the charge and without having seemed to move, I was standing on the blood-slick deck where arrow-stuck bodies lay about. My nausea was forgotten, Hwyl was in my fist and the familiarity of skirmishing was washing over me.

A mariner ran at me with a pike and I swung my blade, deflecting the shaft and the gleaming axe head, then looped the steel around in a full circle. It smashed into the man's knee, shattering it and dropping him to the deck. I glanced at his face, his lips already pain-grey as he rocked in agony, his arms sheeted with bright blood and wrapped around his shattered limb. No more threat from this one. I moved on.

Two French sailors armed only with knives backed up, then scuttled away, and I found myself facing a dark-visaged knight in purple surcoat with a boar's head emblem. He poked out his sword in an oddly tentative manner, half defensive, half the offer of a gift. I simply swept it clattering into the scuppers. He immediately dropped to his knees, in probably the fastest submission I had ever enjoyed. "Je me rends," he said simply, showing me his palms and shrugging his

shoulders expressively. I scooped up his sword, glanced at it
– no goldwork, a cheap looking blade – and threw it over the
side. I'd claim him later, for the ransom. For now, back to the
fighting...

The noise of battle was deafening. Our men bellowed hoarse,
loud war cries over the screams of the wounded and the clang
of metal on metal. An ominous drift of smoke caught in my
nostrils. Around me, French sailors were diving through the
hatchways to hide, five or six of their knights were back to
back, encircled by the pikes of the boarders from FitzJohn's
ship and a dozen or more knights were meekly handing over
their swords to the English. It was all as quick as that.

In minutes those on deck were secured and herded under
guard to the forecastle and a pack of our men at arms was
clattering down the hatchways and plunging into the bowels
of the ship like hounds after an otter. I always wondered about
that: in a ship fight or when a fortification fell, some men
scuttled to dark recesses to hide. It never worked, they were
invariably hunted down, and the chances were enhanced of
them being quietly dispatched by a blood-lusting soldier who
was away from the gaze of his commanders. Better to stay on
the deck or the ramparts and die in the open, or surrender if
you must, but at least die in daylight.

Suddenly the noise changed. The bellowed war cries, the
shouts and grunts and clashing metal of fighting men had

ended. Now what was to be heard were muted screams from below, and on the blood-pooled deck, only the groans of the wounded and the death rattles of those exhaling their last. An English captain was shouting for water to douse a fire – the one thing both sets of fighting men most feared on these tinderbox wooden ships.

Someone hauled down Courtenay's crimson and gold banner from the topmast, though we did not have our own with which to replace it. The action was a signal for the whole French fleet, which had curiously been maintaining position a bowshot's distance away without coming to the aid of their flagship, to turn and flee towards France. Our warships, lean and fast, were onto the clumsy, wallowing troopships like wolves on a wounded stag.

Aboard the Bayonne, our blood-maddened men were through the hatches, eager for victims. As usual, no mercy was afforded to the cowering French mariners and men at arms, who were hunted through the dimness below decks, and only a few of whom were dragged up alive to see daylight. Among them was the monk Eustace, still in the hooded black scapular of a Benedictine. He was soaked and stinking of shit. "Hiding deep in the bilge, sire," I heard one of his captors tell FitzJohn. The monk was on his knees now, speaking rapidly, offering the vast ransom of 10,000 marks for his life.

FitzJohn spat in Eustace's face and the gabble halted. "You

were employed by my father and you betrayed him," he said. "You sacked and burned English towns, you took English men and women and sold them as slaves. There is no mercy for a whore like you, who faithlessly services anyone with silver to pay."

The earl looked around. A burly man at arms called Stephen Crabbe, who carried a broad-bladed axe caught his eye. "Fasten this creature to that, and cut off his head," he commanded, gesturing at the gunwale. So Eustace, the monk who turned to piracy, ended his days lashed to his own ship's rail before his head was hacked free and splashed into the waters where he had marauded. A handful of sailors gathered at the rail, laughing at the bobbing head. "Learning to swim are ye?" one shouted. "Don't stop now you're ahead!" The roar of laughter drew a captain's attention and he ordered the men back to work, but I noticed that he too grinned at the jest.

That execution also killed Prince Louis' hopes of conquering England. His supply routes across the Channel were denied him, for we chased down, rammed, sank or captured all but a dozen or so of his fleet. "He only got to keep those few because our sailors were too busy looting the supply ships," said Adam later.

A month after the sea battle, Louis renounced his claims, signed a treaty and left Dover for good with a departure bribe of 10,000 marks from fines levied on the now-pardoned rebel barons. As a strategic matter, my seigneur Earl Ranulf of Chester, who had added the title and castle of Earl of Lincoln to his holdings, was ordered to slight Mountsorrel Castle and with the assistance of the locals completely razed it to the ground.

So, by late 1217, the disaffected rebel barons were back in the fold, the greybeard William Marshal was regent, our king was nine year old Henry of Winchester and the war was over. For now.

Chapter IV: Ramon Alaric

William Marshal was popular, you had to grant that to him. The old warrior who was regent for Henry of Winchester, our new king, crowned at the ripe old age of nine, was well-enough regarded even by the barons and earls who were unsure that they wanted his ward, King John's son, as the new ruler.

"We had a raw time of it with Lackland," said my father bluntly. "He was a grasping, greedy, lecherous little bastard and I expect his son won't be much better. The apple doesn't fall far from the tree."

Adam of Lonsdale, my father's confessor, former tutor and an unexpectedly martial monk, spoke up. "Frederick," he softly told his one-time pupil, "beware you don't speak treason. Walls have ears, especially in this place. And anyway," he said, raising his voice slightly, "Marshal says the new king will rule according to the precepts of Magna Carta."

I glanced around. Adam had a nose like a vixen's for scratching out secrets. What he said aloud meant something. We were in a stone anteroom of the old palace of Winchester, the child-king's birthplace and residence. "Henry might make a good king," I ventured, though I didn't really believe it.

Frederick knew it. He spat into the grate where a sullen fire smouldered. "Old Henry was a middling king," he said, referring to the second of the Plantagenets of that name to rule England. "He had plenty of faults. His son Henry the Young King was a wastrel and it was best he died before his father did so he never got to rule, even though they crowned him. This third Henry got the crown but he comes from bad seed and he is far too young to solve the problems we have."

Frederick looked around cautiously before he continued in a quieter voice. "William Marshal is a decent enough old soldier, but I do not trust Longsword, he has changed his colours too often and too easily. I know he's not officially a regent but he's Old Henry's bastard, which makes him Lackland's half-brother and what, Henry of Winchester's uncle or some such?"

Adam murmured: "Whatever he is, my lord the Earl of Salisbury has certainly just been appointed High Sheriff of Devon to add to his sheriffdoms of Wiltshire and Cambridge. His influence grows and rides tall. Our friend Longsword has taken his place at high table, and Marshal won't be unseating him." I saw that Adam stroked his left forearm, where a knife was strapped, concealed under the sleeve. I'd seen the gesture before and it was something the old warrior-monk did when he was nervous. I suspected his antenna was twitching at the hint of treason. Longsword was a dangerous foe.

A thunder of footsteps in the hall outside caused us to

halt our talk, and the heavy door groaned open as several mailed soldiers strode in behind the tall figure of Jacquin de Grimshaw, a Lancashire baron who was an ordained Templar knight. I recognized Berlage St Denys and William de Vesci of Alnwick. His father Eustace had been a leader of the rebellion against John until he was killed by an arrow strike a year ago.

Behind them was a strong-jawed man with a prominent nose, a kindly eye and blond hair bristle-cut *en brosse* in the French style. He was obviously a man of some import and wore a surplice of blue and gold heavily embroidered in gold thread that featured what I would learn were the arms of Toulouse and the regional red cross of Languedoc.

De Vesci introduced him. "This, gentlemen, is Count Ramon of Toulouse, Marquis of Provence, Count of Melgueil. He is a grandson of Louis of France yet he has been cruelly treated by Rome and has been exiled for being an honest and cultured man." I heard Adam's sharp intake of breath. As usual the monk was ahead of us all in his lightning-quick thinking, and also as usual he had the benefit of an ecclesiastical spy network second to none. His spy network told him things as fast as a polecat smelled danger from her lair. The Frenchman standing before us was the man the powerful northern barons wanted as king in place of the boy Henry.

Count Ramon was speaking with Frederick, and I drew Adam aside to whisper urgently: "What in God's name is he doing here, in Henry's palace?" Adam smiled.

"Where safer?" he asked. "The rebel barons will protect him. They are here, paying lip-service to young Henry, all the while planning to replace him and Longsword and Marshal with this French lord until Henry comes of age. The agreement is already made. Ramon is powerful enough to bring the barons to heel until Henry is ready to fully assume the throne. The count is a pious man and he swears he will step aside at that time."

Adam glanced around to be sure we were not overheard. "The herald Kevin of Carsgrove who keeps the Roll of Arms says that the marks of cadency track a lineage that gives Ramon a legitimate claim to the English throne. He has royal blood, he has a true right to the crown. Ramon has met the leaders of the rebel barons and they are convinced he will serve faithfully and will keep his oaths to relinquish the throne to Henry of Winchester when he is old enough."

I shook my head. "How can this really happen?" I whispered. Adam gestured with his chin. "Obvious. The rebels under de Vesci over there want an end to civil war because it threatens their holdings. Equally, they don't want the French trying another invasion and bringing their Norman and Angevin cronies here to strip us of our lands. So, the barons will cooperate. Ramon is God-sworn to keep his promise to step down in favour of Henry, or he will face the further wrath of Rome and be pushed out. The Pope can call a crusade for the religious orders of the martial knights like the Templars, Hospitallers and the Teutons and all the rest to restore our ordained monarch. They are powerful enough to do it, and they'd strip the barons of their lands and wealth if they did, so it's in the rebels' interest to sustain Ramon.

"Above all that, the Pope also has the power of an interdict up his embroidered sleeve." I nodded. I recalled the stories of when Lackland John was faced down by the Pope, when the dead lay unburied and the dying were unshriven, when every soul in England faced the threat of eternal hellfire. It was all because the king, and by extension his country, suffered the Pope's ill-will and he ordered the clergy not to perform confessions, masses, last rites or burials. I shuddered at the memory.

Across the anteroom, Frederick was in conversation with Ramon and de Vesci. Grimshaw saw my look and moved towards me. "You know what is happening?" he asked quietly.

I nodded. "We're offering him the crown?"

Grimshaw looked around, startled at my blunt summation. "Aye," he said, "but keep that quiet for now. We have to plan the where and when of it all."

That made sense. Winchester was not the place, but walled and warded London was, with its stronghold Tower guarding the first place at which the great Thames could be bridged, with its situation at the heart of the spiderweb of England's roads and, most importantly with its citizens who had welcomed the barons who rebelled against John. London was a commune, self-governing and almost independent of royalty with its folkmoots and courts of husting. This would be the right place to declare a replacement king, even were he only a temporary regent.

Grimshaw was looking at me in a curious manner. "You know we'd have to convince the Londoners that the Articles of the Barons will work for them, too?" I knew. I'd read the great charter and it was no statement of liberties for the common people, it was a deed to limit the king's ability to use his feudal rights to milk the nobles, halting his merciless drive to tax the nobility. Along the way, it also held him answerable to justice.

Lackland, scrabbling for silver, had sold judgements for bribes, just as his father Henry had profitably done. This, the barons tried to stop. They – we – were the beneficiaries, but to get wider support for the rebellion against the king, the charter extended its clauses to cover free men, too. They, but not the unfree, semi-slave villeins who worked the land, could no longer be taken or imprisoned except by the lawful judgement of their peers.

Cornered, John had set his seal to the demands, which were backed by a congress of 25 barons who could lawfully move against the king if he reneged. Which, with Pope Innocent's blessing, he quickly did, and it caused the civil war we were struggling to end. For now, the hostilities were ceasing, as Louis had returned to France, but the coronation of a child king unsettled the powerful men of England, and we wanted Ramon of Toulouse as our temporary ruler. He was here, and we were readying our *coup de main* when Earl Ranulf de Blondeville came on the scene.

Chapter V: Ranulf
Alaric

How he heard about it, I can only guess, although I suspect the monk Walter of Pinchbeck was the informant, for the Earl some years later appointed him abbot, and it may have been a reward. Both were slippery men. However it happened, the plot to supplant Henry with Ramon was fully known to our sworn overlord Earl Ranulf of Chester and he was less than pleased with Frederick and me.

He had us cornered in his chamber at Winchester, where he had summoned us. It must have been an odd sight: Frederick is a big, battle-scarred warrior, I am even bigger and Ranulf is a small, almost petite man, but he was baying at us like a boarhound as we pressed ourselves away from him and against the cold granite of the chamber wall.

The fact is, we both truly liked our overlord, and were torn at being disloyal to him, for he was through and through a king's man. "This is treachery, you are traitors to your own king!" he spluttered. "How can you even consider this plot. I should hand you over to Longspee right this minute." At the mention of Longsword, my spine stiffened. I faced down the man who had been a father to me before I knew who my real father was.

"I should gut that turning, wriggling bastard," I growled at Ranulf. "You call us traitors, but we have never changed sides. Longsword is like a windvane and turns by the hour!"

Ranulf paused. I had never defied him before, and we shared a great affection. I seized the moment. "Ranulf, lord, this is just to put an end to civil strife until Henry is fit to take the throne. Maybe Marshal is trustworthy, but he is an old man and Longsword might become sole regent if he dies. You know you cannot fully trust the slippery Earl of Salisbury. We must remove from him the chance to seize power for himself and his Norman and Angevin cousins!

"We simply want a regent we can trust, and Ramon is a pious, an honourable man." I paused, seeing doubt in Ranulf's face. "His wife was Jeanne of England, which made him kin to three English kings: Lionheart, John and their father Henry. He is related to the King of France and to the King of Aragon. The Raimondines are a noble house and rule well. He would be a fine regent, and we will do it with papal blessing.

"We even have a warranty: should Ramon fail us, we can call out the martial knights, the Templars, on a holy crusade to restore Henry. I'll even become a Templar myself so I can better persuade my own brotherhood to do it!" As the words fell from my mouth, I knew I was forecasting my future, my purpose in life. I would become a religious knight, dedicated to God and right. My life was set.

Ranulf knew it for a genuine, inspired sentiment. "I too have made such a vow," he said. "In 1215 I vowed I would take the Cross and go on crusade. I will honour my promise, and I am impressed that you have seen your calling to God." My father, wily old rogue that he is, considered my blurted admission as a mere ploy to sway Ranulf's judgement and I felt his elbow nudge my ribs. I turned to remonstrate, thought better of it and clamped shut my lips.

Ranulf misread the action and thought I was seeking Frederick's approval. He spoke hurriedly. "You have my blessing, as well as that of your father, eh Frederick?"

That worthy nodded judiciously. "Well done, my boy," he said blandly. "Let us discuss the Templars. And, my lord," a small bow to Ranulf, "you might wish to speak with Count Ramon and hear his story for yourself."

So, two days later, we heard the full tale of the cruel, bloody Cathar wars that had already raged across southern France for nearly a decade. It was a story Ramon had told me once before, but it was a powerful recounting of evil that transfixed us all.

Ramon sat at a table littered with a clerk's scrolls and inkpots, fixed us with his steady, unswerving gaze and said: "I swear to the veracity of what I am going to tell you. There have been unbelievable cruelties committed in the name of Christ, some of them authorized by the pope himself in his bid to become the feudal overlord of the world. Happily that pope, Innocent III, has gone to his eternal fate, but evil is still being perpetrated across my lands and on my innocent people."

He was, he claimed, a good Catholic, but Ramon's second wife – he was married six times – had become a Cathar *parfaite*, a member of the elite of the sect, and many of his subjects followed the creed so he was sympathetic to it.

"The word Cathar means 'pure,'" the count explained, "and the Cathars, the *bonhommes*, are ascetics who believe in austerity and in renouncing worldly pleasures. Cathar priests teach that the Devil creates pleasure and that God creates pure souls who must resist pleasures in this life. Souls are angels trapped in human form and are reincarnated until we gain redemption. Believers may marry, *parfaits* must stay celibate. Most, shortly before they die, undergo the baptism of *consolamentum* to purify their souls and gain salvation."

The wealthy Languedoc cities of Toulouse and Albi were centres of Catharism, so many of the count's subjects followed the creed, which was condemned as heresy by the Catholic Church. This caused conflict for Ramon, who held Provence as a vassal of the Holy Roman Emperor and who was ordered to put down the heretics whom he counted as his subjects. "Ten years ago, the Pope ordered the Dominicans to conduct a preaching campaign against my people. It failed, and a papal legate, an arrogant Cistercian who accused me of abetting

51

heresy, excommunicated me.

"I admit we quarrelled, and fiercely. However it happened, the fellow was killed as he returned to his master in Rome. For this, Pope Innocent held me responsible and took his chance to intervene in southern France, to seize control of lands which rightly belonged to the king. He let loose the dangerous dogs of the north, and authorised them to plunder.

"The pope did not forget my part, either. Later, I was subjected to public humiliations which I had to accept on pain of forfeiting my eternal soul."

Ramon, overlord of the land, was led naked and barefoot through the streets of Saint-Gilles to the church gates, forced to swear on the body of Christ and an assortment of holy relics that he would be obedient to Rome, then was scourged as penance.

Pope Innocent proclaimed a crusade against the 'sinister race' of Languedoc, ordering them exterminated 'root and branch.' He offered spiritual indulgences and the remission of sins for those who answered his call and declared that the lands and treasure of the heretics would be forfeit to the crusaders.

"There was a flood of knights from northern France," Ramon said bitterly. "They came not for religious purposes, but to rape, plunder and steal. The most devilish of them was Simon de Montfort, to whom the Pope has now ceded my estates."

De Montfort took fire and sword to the Cathars. He sacked the city of Beziers, slaughtering more than 7,000 townspeople, only 200 or so of whom were Cathars. When the spiritual advisor to the crusade, the papal legate Arnaud-Almauric of Citeaux was asked about how the crusaders could tell Catholics from heretics, the blood-lusting abbot shouted: "Kill them all. God will know His own!" The soldiery reacted with gusto. Citizens, even children were used for target practice, were dragged behind horses, were blinded, mutilated and killed.

At the siege of Carcassonne, the water supply was cut off and the citizens surrendered. They were allowed to leave for exile with just the clothes they wore, 'taking nothing but their sins' while their leaders were tortured and hanged. The fortress of Minerve also fell when its water supply was cut. The Cathar defenders were forcibly converted to Catholicism, except for 140 who refused and were burned at the stake.

When the citadel of Bram fell to de Montfort, he ordered the mutilation of every member of the Cathar garrison that had resisted him. Each soldier had his eyes gouged out and his nose and upper lip cut off. Just one man was left with a single sighted eye, and he was ordered to lead the others to the next citadel, to inspire fear. De Montfort routinely employed branding, burning, hanging, crushing, pillorying and breaking on the wheel to obtain information, to locate buried riches or simply to cow the local population. By and large, it worked. Town after town meekly opened their gates to his troops, handing over their Cathar fellow citizens to torture and death.

"Because of my oath to the Pope, I had to ride with these crusaders and do battle with my own people," said Ramon. "It broke my heart, but my eternal soul was at risk. Finally, I could stand it no longer and I slipped away to organise resistance when de Montfort went to besiege my citadel at Toulouse. He set fires, but we blocked him in the streets with great wooden beams and wine casks and met force with force."

One thing worked in Ramon's favour. The pope required only 40 days' military service of his crusaders to earn God's blessing, so the loot-inspired horde that went south for the summer campaign season turned around after six weeks and left de Montfort greatly weakened.

He was still strong enough to capture the castle at Lavaur that was the stronghold of Aimery de Montreal. That knight and his 80 soldiers were all hanged on one huge gibbet, which collapsed under the strain. De Montfort ordered his men to slash the soldiers' throats as they lay stunned among the wreckage. Next, he had the 400 Cathar captives burned, and then the victor ordered the defeated lord's sister Giralda de Laurac to be gang-raped by his crusaders before she was thrown down a well and stoned to death.

The horrors continued. At Casses, 50 Cathars were burned;

at Termes, Cathar forces cut de Montfort's crusader rear-guard to pieces and vengefully mutilated every captive. The crusaders continued their war of terror, burning 80 heretics in Strasburg, butchering the villagers of Ananclet, burning down Auterive on suspicion it was a Cathar centre, and besieging Hautpol and Moissac before massacring the inhabitants, some by throwing them from the town walls.

Even the dead and buried were not immune to the cruelties of the war. De Montfort's men exhumed Cathar corpses so they could burn the bodies. "They want every trace of us gone," said Ramon, and we sat in stunned silence as the count iterated the toll of rape and murder that the pope had inspired and that de Montfort had carried out.

"King Philippe was so pressured by the pope, he even sent his son Prince Louis to aid de Montfort. In turn Simon paid homage to the king, ceding his conquests – including my lands – to the French crown. I have been exiled, but I am going back. I can call on my cousins in Aragon for help, but if you care to assist me against plunderers and a venal pope, I shall be grateful."

Frederick bowed his head, then raised it to look Ramon square in the eyes. "When I heard that the pope had called for a crusade against the Cathars, I saw it as my duty to go. Years before, I went with my friend and king, Lionheart, to fight the Saracens. We had some great victories, Deus Vult, and crusading may have earned me a key to heaven. Now, what you tell me, and what I know of Rome convinces me that a crusade against those men of Provence and Languedoc would be wrong. I cannot in conscience bear arms against them. Even at the risk of my soul, I cannot agree that what the pope ordered is right in God's eyes."

To me, it made sense. The pope had made a blatant, un-Christian grab for power. Frederick was speaking again. He wondered aloud if the Cathars could resist the might of Rome and the might of the French king. Ramon smiled quietly and told us of a wealthy Toulousian magistrate, a respected old man called Pierre Maurand who was uncovered as a Cathar and, sentenced to death, offered to convert to save his life.

"He was taken from prison and compelled to walk barefoot to the church of Saint-Raumes while the bishop and a legate beat him with rods," said Ramon. "At the church, he was forced to kneel and beg forgiveness, his houses were ordered destroyed and his goods confiscated, then he was commanded to go to Jerusalem and for three years to serve the holy city's poor.

"Before he left, so that all in the city would know he had recanted, he was to spend 40 days wandering naked from church to church, scourging himself all the while.

"Maurand came back after his exile and defiantly resumed his secret preaching of Catharism," said Ramon. "For five consecutive periods of three years, my fellow citizens re-elected him consul of the city, an honour to mark his resistance to a foreign pope. That is the kind of men who are the Cathars. If you come, you will find willing recruits to the cause. De Montfort will not prevail."

Chapter VI: Treasure
Alaric

There was much to do before we could leave for the
Languedoc. We had to secure the crown regalia that we had
hidden in Lincolnshire and get some of it into Ramon's
hands to help validate his claim to the English throne. I had
to be inducted into the Templar order and I wanted to make
arrangements about the vast sum of gold that Frederick had
liberated from King John's treasury.

I knew that the Templars were not only one of the world's
best-disciplined and effective fighting forces, thanks to their
strictly-enforced vows of obedience, but the fighting friars
also wielded considerable political power and had developed
moneylending and banking interests.

Their compound by the Fleet river in London was used
as a place of safety for jewels, documents and silver, and a
merchant or noble could deposit money there, receive a letter
of credit for it and carry that document safely across Europe
to cash it in at another Templar treasury a thousand miles away.

"The brethren in Paris are King Louis' own bankers," said
Sir John Gardiner proudly. "We are entrusted with his royal
gold, and I hear we even keep his kingly regalia and jewels

safe, too." He went on to confide that the order made loans to other royal houses, not least the kings of Aragon, although he ruefully admitted: "sometimes we're stretched to meet the royal demands and have to borrow money ourselves. It's not always easy to stay in the royal favour, and turning down a request for a loan is a good way to fall from grace." But, he added, the gold always came back. Kings made good debtors and repaid the Templars because they always needed to call on their creditors again.

All of this convinced me that I should entrust to the order the huge fortune my father had liberated from King John's hoard, so I went to visit Frederick to talk about matters.

He nodded vigorously when I outlined my thoughts. "You are right to save your soul, and becoming a Templar will guarantee that. I expect we'll be joining Ramon on his expedition to France – eh?"

"Yes, father," I said. "It seems to be the right thing to do. The new pope cannot be as land-hungry as Innocent was. It is wrong that Rome wants to steal Louis' fiefs, it seems to me. We should go and send de Montfort back home."

Frederick tugged at his beard. "I'll be happier when we have the regalia secured. We should move everything from Donington. You take the gold to London, I'll get the crown jewels to Chester, to Abbot Hugh, and it will also be under the unknowing guardianship of Earl Ranulf." The knight Berlage

St Denys was in the chamber with us as we spoke and he raised an eyebrow. Frederick saw the query and snorted. "Of course, old friend, we kept this secret even from you. Well, it's time others knew more…

"King John planned to pawn the royal regalia and contrived a plot with the moneylender Jews of Norwich, but it went wrong when his baggage train was swamped in the tidal marshes of the Wash. John had made me Jewel Master and with a few of the barons, we had a plan to liberate what regalia we would need to crown our new, legitimate king once we had deposed John.

"Well, things worked out beautifully, I was able to acquire not only the regalia we needed – including the Holy Roman Empress' crown – but also made off with a fine collection of jewels and a fortune in gold ingots. The best part of it all is that everyone thinks that John's treasures are under the mud and tides of the Wash, but actually they are concealed in a burial vault in a church at Donington, near Newark."

I took in Berlage's expression. His jaw was open, his eyes wide. "You have the crown jewels and a fortune besides?" he said incredulously.

Frederick smirked, there was no other word for it. "Enough to make any coronation a legitimate one, and enough to fund an army to sustain a king of our choosing."

Berlage's eyes narrowed. "And, Frederick, whom do you

choose?" he said quietly.

Frederick glanced at me. "Ask Alaric," he said. "It is his generation and that of my grandsons who will select their king. All we do now is secure the throne by putting a trustworthy regent in place to hold it for Henry of Winchester."

So it was with our mission defined that Frederick and I rode to a small place in Lincolnshire midway between the site of the disaster at the Wash and the priory at Swineshead where the fevered King John had been taken afterwards. In a sealed vault of Donington's Church of St Mary and the Holy Rood lay six leather panniers heavy with a king's stolen treasure. Adam of Lonsdale had chosen the hiding place, as he knew a young monk there, one Walter from the nearby village of Pinchbeck. He also knew that Lackland John had burdened the abbey and many others with intolerable taxes that had stripped the community of its wealth. An enemy of John's would be a friend of the monks, and as Adam expected, the old abbot, gently introduced to the idea by Walter, was eager to cooperate although he did not know exactly what it was that he was hiding.

So, one blustery October night we had sealed the treasure inside an unused tomb – the church was only 20 years old and had plenty of space – and there it had lain for more than a year. I sent messages to Isaac of Norwich, the moneylender who wanted to purchase John's jewels and Frederick and I, with a considerable entourage of mailed men at arms, rode across the limestone hills of central England to retrieve the treasures.

As we rode, Frederick told me what was contained in those leather panniers. "There's the crown, the finest of them, the coronation crown of the Holy Roman Empress Matilda," he said in an odd sing-song voice. As he continued, I realized that he had memorised the list and had spoken it to himself many times. He continued: "The crown was the first thing I considered when I was cherry-picking the jewels to steal, because it was the most important crown. It has the added virtue of being lightweight and cunningly made in seven hinged segments so it can be packed flat for travelling.

"Even its traveling case is special: it is made from linden wood taken from a tree in the courtyard of the imperial castle at Nuremberg, a tree that was planted by the Empress Cunigunde, wife of Henry II, a full century before Empress Matilda's birth.

"The crown is a glittering confection of jewels and gold. The front displays a setting of purple amethysts, ice-blue sapphires and ocean-green emeralds that frame three magnificent blood-red rubies the size of plover's eggs." I looked across at him as we trotted tranquilly along the Roman road of Watling Street, one of the four great highways of Britain that enjoyed the security of the King's Peace. His eyes were closed as he recited the inventory. "The crown is further topped with a golden cross studded with jewels and more than 100 large pearls fill every conceivable part of the structure. Finally, a band of ermine and velvet cushions the wearer's brow.

His eyes were still closed, he was unaware of his horse's jolting pace. "With it goes the sacred Anointing Spoon and the solid gold flask of oil in the shape of an eagle; the long, bejeweled sword that legend says once belonged to Tristram. There is the royal Sceptre of Virtue, an ivory and gold baton topped with the dove of peace; the great ruby Ring of Unity and the heavy, ivory-ebony-and-gold Orb of Dominion that signifies Our Lord Christ's power over the world, to be passed on to the anointed one who will be His earthly representative.

"Lastly there is the dalmatic robe of red-gold silk threaded with gold and stiff with emeralds, rubies and sapphires, all sewn into its seams and facings."

He opened his eyes but still seemed far away. We paced our horses for minutes in silence, then I asked: "And the gold, and jewels?" Frederick blinked and wiped at his eyes.

"Yes, lots of that, lots of it," he said. "The gold is mostly ingots, small ingots, very heavy, they fill two panniers. There's enough to build a half-dozen abbeys and their supporting farms, I suppose." He visibly shook himself. The gold was not so important to him, his mind was on the sacred regalia, but I was insistent.

"And the jewels, Frederick?"

"Oh yes, they're worth more than all the gold put together," he said, off-handedly. "John was a terrible hoarder, a miser, really. He coveted jewels and would confiscate them from his courtiers if they were unwise enough to wear them to court. Sometimes the great nobles would deliberately flaunt their finest jewels, knowing the king would grab them, but it would earn them some favour, or at least save them from harm for a short while."

Frederick paused, considering: "I had some luck, too. John had called a congress to manage his royal forests at Epping and Dean and wanted a regal display for the Welsh and some of the ladies he planned to seduce, so had his finest jewels taken to his lodge at St Briavel's Castle. Happily for me, he still had them with him in East Anglia."

He leaned forward to pat his palfrey's neck. "Yes, the jewels are magnificent. Rings, brooches, bracelets, pendants, only a few bits of religious artefacts. I took the best jewels because I wanted to liquidate them, get gold for them, and the Jews have little use for Christian bishops' crosses and the like. Unmounted jewels weigh little, and are worth much, and there's a whole leather pannier full of the things. It was a most rewarding perquisite of being the royal Jewel Master and being prepared when disaster strikes.

"I met Isaac, you know. He was leaving the courtyard at the

priory as I rode in that night. John was too ill to complete his business with him but we'll finish the brokerage this week, he and I."

So it was settled. I would take most of the gold to London and the Templars and prepare myself to receive my Templar spurs. Privately, I planned to keep some gold back for future use. I went over the plan again. Frederick would turn the jewels into gold, with Isaac of Norwich's help, and take the royal regalia to Chester to be immured by Abbot Hugh until the time was right. "I'll need some of the regalia for Ramon, father," I said, "something to show him we mean to support him."

"Yes, yes, Alaric," he said a little absently, I thought. "I'll get something to you. Don't worry about it."

Chapter VII: Sword
Frederick

Alaric's a fine boy, a man, really, but he can be a bit naïve. I suppose it's all this business about getting religion, following in his mother's footsteps. I've been an indulgence-granted crusader, and fought and killed Saracens while shouting God's name, but nobody has ever said to me: "Frederick, you're a religious example to us all." Fact is, I have a silver *mjollnir* – the short-handled hammer of Thor – on a chain hidden under my tunic. It's an ancient thing, a pagan talisman of some long-dead warrior, I expect, and it's a sort of nod to the ancient gods because, God or man, you can never trust anyone very much, and it pays to keep your options open.

The same goes for Ramon of Toulouse. He might be a fine French fellow and we could certainly use him to stabilise the throne, but I would not just deliver to him a sacred relic that gave his claims the aura of legitimacy without being fully sure of the fellow. I've seen too many people change sides, and too often. What if we handed over the sacred regalia of England and the fellow didn't play straight with us? I thought it through, and decided that the thing to do would be to use an old tactic and give him a fake relic. If he were honest, nothing would come of it. If he were being slippery and devious, then we could always point out that his claim to legitimacy was based on a falsehood and discredit him. Just keeping my options open, you see.

It was the obvious answer, to me anyway, and I resolved to give him a replica of the coronation sword, the fabled Sword of Tristan. How would he know if it was real or not? It would satisfy him, keep Alaric quiet in his new religious thinking and the true power would stay where it belonged, with the northern barons who opposed John. Like me they have their doubts about the regent and the uncle pulling the puppet strings of John's son and heir. Because the regalia was kept locked away except for ceremonial occasions, nobody really, except the late Lackland and myself as Jewel Master, had properly had the chance to examine the sword closely. Any decent facsimile would do the trick.

And, remembering other religious icons, we might usefully create an extra one or two, while we were about it. Of course, I'd let a few of my fellow jarls in on the secret, but my boy Alaric was a bit too godly and upstanding to keep such a trick quiet. Best he didn't know about things…

So it was that Alaric and I retrieved the treasures from the monks of Donington, and a quiet sigh of regret escaped the abbot when we did. I slipped him a couple more gold ingots, showed him my teeth in an unconvincing smile and patted my sword hilt meaningfully. He paled a little at the threat of Bloodblade and hastened to tell me how our secret was safe with him, by God's teeth, my lord.

Alaric took the road south, headed for London and the Templars and I turned my cavalcade northwest, but only for a mile or so. I pulled up my palfrey in a little grove of trees, gestured for the troopers to send out sentries and secure the area, and slid from the saddle. I walked back to where the four troopers each had a packhorse tethered to his own nag and I scanned the bundles tightly fastened to the sumpters that were nibbling an unexpected snack of damp grass.

"Unfasten that one," I pointed at a longish package, and a man at arms loosened the bindings. Inside the leather as I expected it to be was Tristram's sword. "Wrap it up again," I said. "Will," I pointed at a grizzled old cavalryman who had been with me at Acre all those years before. "Dismount and walk with me a moment." We strode away, out of hearing of the curious troopers.

I pulled a folded parchment from my gauntlet. "Keep this safe. You're to deliver it and the sword to the smith Burrjust at his forge in Bents Green. It is near Sheffield in my lord of Hallamshire's fief. The paper tells him what to do."

I was confident that Will, weathered and hardened soldier that he was, would not be able to comprehend the French and Latin I had used to keep my instructions confidential, not that

I thought he would even attempt to read them. Burrjust was equally trustworthy. A literate monk who had apprenticed to the famed smith Weland of Kent before he went back home to Yorkshire, I had first come across the burly cleric when he delivered a cartload of arrowheads to Ranulf's castle.

He had repaired some small pieces of armour for me and had also created a beautiful punching knife which I kept concealed in a lanolin-greased sheath at the nape of my neck. He was the craftsman I needed for this special and discreet task. Will was tucking the parchment, folded small, into his belt pouch. "Wait, Will," I said. "You should also put this in there." I handed him a small leather purse of silver. "Give half to the smith, tell him there will be plenty more when he delivers his work to me at Bank Hall. Use the rest for your men. Take three trusted ones with you, make sure they can keep their mouths shut firm. If word leaks, I shall have them hanged. All of them."

Will nodded. He knew me, he expected as much and he knew that my own trust in him excluded him from the threat. "Aye, I'll do that all right, lord," he said.

"Cross the Trent at Newark, where John died," I instructed, "then strike north and west across the Peak on the old Roman road. It's just three days of easy travel and stay out of the taverns until you have delivered all. Carry on to Chester when you're done. I'll see you there."

I had other business, too. A week before, in conversation with my old crusader comrade Berlage St Denys, he had detailed an unusual dream that had come to him. "It started with Longsword," he said. "I saw him on a catafalque, laid out and dead, with his hands folded across his chest, resting on the hilt of his crusader sword. He was not in mail, but wearing a shroud, and in moments he was suddenly a skeleton and there was a dead rat curled inside his skull. Oddly, although his flesh had vanished, the shroud remained as new and untouched as in the first image I had of him. I am sure it was a message from heaven."

My mind drifted. He was fey, my warrior friend. Once, as we rode across the great plain on the south of England and passed the mysterious Standing Stones, he had said something casually about them being moved with music and dance from far away. I had almost ignored the remark, but something made me ask what he meant. "Oh," he said half-dreamily, "they were another thing elsewhere. They made them, you know, with wood and water." It irritated me. Testily, I asked him what he meant.

"Well," he said as if he were looking at something I could not see, "the stones were formed. They just had to be liberated from their rest." I shook my head, still irritated.

"Like Longsword at rest?" I said, tartly.

Berlage was staring at me. "No," he said. "Attend to the

signs." I gave up, I couldn't understand what he was half-dreaming about. He always was a spiritual person, seeking omens in the flight of birds or the mutter and boom of summer thunder, and this shroud dream had impressed him. A shroud, I thought, what could be so holy about it? Especially a shroud on that reprobate Longsword?

"Why would the shroud be holy?" I asked Berlage.

"I meditated on this," he said, "and I think it was a sign that God wraps us in his goodness, and even a sinner like Longsword can be saved. The rat symbolised death and corruption, the shroud was Christ's protection for us."

That started my thoughts racing. Protection, a religious icon to reassure the troops that Christ was with his soldiers. What could be a better banner or shield than to have the very shroud that had once wrapped Christ's holy body? Where could I find it? Did I even need to find it? If men could be inspired to follow saintly relics like the hand of Saint James, a severed hand which I had noted was not the one missing from his body in its Compostela shrine, then they would rally behind the image of Christ on his winding sheet. All I needed was to get one made… The thought took deep root, and I acted on it. Now it was time to set the plan in motion.

As we sat our mounts in the shelter of that leafy copse, I waved over another man at arms, an intelligent fellow I'd noted in the past. From my gauntlet I pulled out a second, folded

piece of vellum. "Take this message to the weaver Nickell
at his house in Hurcott. It's a small place near Kideminstre,
you'll have to ask directions when you get closer. The manor is
owned by the Bisets, I know them and you can ask their help
if you have difficulties." I gave this man, too, a leather purse of
silver.

"Nickell is to travel to my hall in Lancastershire where I
have important work for him. He must come with you, even
if you have to bring him at sword point. Take two men with
you and be at Bank Hall within eight days. If the weaver needs
an apprentice with him, he may bring one. Just be sure neither
of them is armed. I want him at the hall, healthy and ready to
work. You can assure him we will have the things he needs for
his labours."

So a sword would go to Ramon as token of the support of
the English barons, but the true sword would stay with me, as
would the Empress' crown and the great ruby ring. These were
the essential heart of the regalia and I was reluctant to commit
them to the care of anyone, even my lord Ranulf and his tame
abbot. I had to take extra precautions over those three vital
items. But first, to deal with the immediate business.

Instructions were given, troopers sent on their different
ways. I had my arrangements to hide the regalia, and to do
business with Isaac. I must also call on a coiner who carried on
his illegal trade in Waleton-le-dale, in my own demesne. I knew

of it, and allowed it as he'd proved useful to me in the past, a matter I did not care to bruit abroad.

Alaric my son, you'd burst your blood if you knew what I was doing, I chuckled. And so would those prating clergy. Nickell the Weaver's work will thrill and delight every one of them, from pope to presbyter, I mused, so long as they never discover the truth. Or how I'm hiding the crown and ruby…

I looked at my depleted escort. I still had nine men, enough to deter any but a very large band of footpads, and even if they outnumbered us by as many as three or four to one, they would fare very badly against these trained and armed troopers. "Right, you men, walk on," I waved the horses forward. To Chester, now.

We had a fortune in treasure, the royal regalia, that would be hidden for now, and another fortune to be spilled across a table for the assessing eyes of a moneylender. Those jewels would convert into booty that I earmarked for my grandsons. It was they who would inherit Bank Hall and its demesnes on my death, for Alaric would be a Templar under sacred orders. A chest or two of gold would equip Thurstan and Robert for whatever they wished in life. Finally, I grinned to myself, there was enough gold for a handsome sum to go to a deserving abbess who happened to be Alaric's mother. It was pleasant to consider that King John's ill-gotten fortune was going to support his own heir's rival and I would be a kingmaker. Life

was good.

Chapter VIII: Spurs
Alaric

Frederick had seemed almost merry when I left him at Donington, as if he had a secret joke he was not sharing. It left me wondering, because he was a grim and usually humourless old soldier, but the demands of the journey and contemplating my future as a militant cleric soon distracted me from the puzzle.

"Lord Alaric, will we be staying with the Templars in their inns?" a trooper asked me as we trotted our beasts over the stone Roman way.

"Probably," I said. "Why do you ask?"

"Well," said the man, looking embarrassed, "except for being in the castle, I have never slept under a stone roof, and I'm afraid of being crushed." The thought gave me pause. England had very few brick or stone buildings, it was an art lost, like that of making smooth roads, since the Romans left. I had seen the magnificent bath at Aquae Sulis, and gaped at the arching Roman domes that roof public buildings in London, but only the new cathedrals and the castles of the nobility were not made of wood.

"We'll find you a safe place to sleep," I promised. "Maybe

we'll billet you in a tavern with a few whores."

The man grinned. "I hear London has those, young and pretty ones, too," he said hopefully, and he turned his horse's head away to resume his place in the line of march.

He left me thinking of my own destiny. As a Templar, I would be devoting my life and my sword Hwyl to God, my faith would be my armour and my oaths of poverty and chastity would be my riches. Almost all my riches, I quietly qualified myself. That amendment pushed aside, I continued my musing. I would have my hair cropped close and wear a plain white woollen tunic as symbol of humility and purity of purpose. I would be an obedient warrior-monk, a soldier for Christ… My life would change. I nudged my courser with my knees, urging him on a little quicker. We had a distance still to ride.

Our journey took us through Cambridge and the Fens, and we came into London's smokiness through the Aldgate north of the hill on which stands the formidable Tower of Duke William. A flock of ravens flew cawing overhead and the troopers made the sign against evil and blessed themselves. "Corpse-eaters, those, lord," one man muttered.

"Scavengers, yes," I said. "No worse than the pigs and kites that clean the streets." Privately, I thought that the ravens would have plenty of corpses to feed on, for the Tower was a place of execution for many. There was even a burning going on now, and we halted to watch.

"She's a bad one, that," said a burly bystander who from his blood-stained apron was likely a butcher. "A witch. Her man died, and she carved him in wood, dressed his clothes on the effigy and trapped his spirit in there. They say the wooden man moved and spoke, and she could commune with the dead to learn secrets."

I shuddered at the evil and in that moment, across the crowd, the woman looked directly at me. She ignored the men who were piling brush and firewood around her bound limbs and addressed me directly and clearly. "You have the treasure," she said. "It is not yours and it is not right." The crowd stirred and some turned to see who it was she addressed. I pulled my horse's head around.

"Move on," I commanded. A shiver ran up my spine.

The troopers murmured a little but at that moment several ravens swooped very low over us, claws scraping our helmets and they waved them away, shouting at the birds. We moved on and the men were soon distracted again, gaping at the towering buildings and at the strength of the brick and tile Roman walls. We clopped through the poulterers' and mercers' streets, crossed the sewer-stinking Walbrook and rode down the hill to exit the city through the Ludgate, where we clattered over the wood-planked Fleet bridge. At that river, the black friars' priory held one bank and the white friars' compound faced them from the other. To our left, alongside the wide Thames, was our destination: the courts and their circular Temple Church so faithfully modelled on the Church of the Holy Sepulchre in Jerusalem.

The Templars' courts were where Lackland had entrusted the royal treasury, and where my father had overseen the handling of the coronation regalia. He had also, as the king's Jewel Master, been responsible for the fortune in jewels that John had amassed. Perhaps it was the witch's challenge, but I gulped at the thought of our temerity at seizing so much of the king's plunder, and mentally apologized to the grotesque, painted stone effigies that looked down on the courtyards and had guarded the lost royal treasure.

The place was more than just a marble-pillared temple and treasury, it was a monastery, a cavalry barracks and a garrison complex of buildings, with splendid residences for the kings and papal legates who stayed here. There were mews and dormitories for the humbler; with facilities for military training and recreation alongside stabling, cooks' quarters, a bakery and storehouses, several wells, armourers' workshops and smiths' forges.

Six or seven porters and burly gatekeepers stepped forward to meet us, eyeing our armed troop warily, so I waved most of my entourage back. Only two troopers were to accompany me and I gestured to the ones who led certain packhorses to bring their burdens. Soon I was ushered into the presence of an almoner clad in the black habit of a Benedictine monk. "I hear you have brought a donation," he began at once. I'd expected it, and waved forward the two troopers who each carried a pair of heavy saddlebags. The ingots inside were carefully layered in silencing linen, but the bags still made a promising clink as they were dumped on the almoner's table. He gave them a dispassionate glance and waved the troopers away.

"You are to become a Templar," he said as greeting. It was not a question. This man does not wrap up his conversation in platitudes, I thought. A nod served as my answer. "This gold will not buy you favour," he said with a little frost in his voice. Again, a nod from me.

Silence, then I thought it best to speak. "I am prepared for a vow of poverty, master." He looked at me with some asperity.

"You will also takes vows of chastity and obedience," he said coldly.

All I could do was to incline my head. This was not beginning well. I had already deceived the order I wanted to join, for although I was handing over a king's ransom, prudence had made me hold back a considerable fortune for my own future use. Not a lot of point mentioning that at this time, I thought wryly. Well, it is hard for a soldier to break the habits of a lifetime. Anyway, an imp of deceit was murmuring in my ear, much of John's gold was ill-gotten and came from fines and fees like merchet, which a wealthy widow had to pay to the king to avoid being married to someone the king chose.

If she failed to pay the typical levy of hundreds of marks, not only would the poor woman have to surrender her body to a stranger forced upon her by the king, but the marriage meant she would also give up control of her wealth and estates. It usually followed that her own children would not inherit, and instead those of her new, forcibly-acquired spouse would assume the fortune. "John never deserved this gold," said the imp. "It is tainted, unworthy of the church. You can use it better…"

The almoner was speaking again and brought me back from my musing. "Let us start with your name," he said, pulling vellum and ink to himself.

"I am Alaric de Banastre," I said. He frowned.

"I heard you were Alaric of Waleton-le-dale."

"Until my real father told me the truth, I was, " I admitted. "Now I am a de Banastre, son of Frederick and of Blanche d'Oate, abbess of Romsey." I had the pleasure of seeing the almoner's pursed lips open in surprise. He stood abruptly, brushed at his habit, muttered something unintelligible and sped from the chamber. I caught the two troopers, who had positioned themselves against the wall, grinning at each other.

"Never knew you were so holy, lord," one said slyly. I shrugged.

"Bless you," I said and they began laughing.

Chapter IX: Isaac
Frederick

My days had been so busy I had to tell myself: "Freddy, take a rest, you're not a pup anymore." I had ridden back to Norwich and met Isaac the Jew, and our negotiations over the glittering mound of jewels accumulated by King John had been civilly brief. Naturally, I had retained some pieces for my own use, mostly jewels and the Christian icons the Jew's clients would not want. Isaac had handed over some gold and two promissory notes for a great deal more to be drawn on the Templars' treasure houses in London and Marseille.

The disposal of the loose jewels complete, I saddled up again and rode hard to Chester only to find my overlord Ranulf de Blondeville not there. "He is on a circuit of his sheriffdoms," explained the castle constable, "he is in Shropshire and will be going on to Lincoln, but your grandsons are here, lord." That brightened my mood. Alaric's sons Thurstan and Robert were training as squires with Earl Ranulf and had been on an expedition into western Wales to subdue bandits who plagued the Conwy valley. They had returned with several gory trophies at their saddlebows just two days before I arrived at the sandstone ramparts of Chester Castle.

The teenagers, both of them tall and dark, greeted me eagerly, and as a proud grandfather I welcomed the opportunity away from Ranulf's presence to inform the boys of the secret I carried. We sat on a bench in a sunny corner of the tiltyard while I briefly outlined matters. "I have a considerable treasure with me," I told them, quietly. "It is the true coronation regalia of England's kings, believed lost or sold by Lackland John. You do not need to know how I came by it, but I have it, and I have other jewels that once were the king's, as well.

"I shall pass some of the regalia into the safekeeping of the monks of Chester without letting Earl Ranulf know. This is because the earl was John's man and was once considered as a possible royal regent of the boy Henry of Winchester. As you know, William Marshal is the official regent, but John's devious half-brother William Longsword shares the duties and is the power behind the throne. Even now he may well try to seize power for himself. To that end, he may invoke loyalty to John, and conscript Ranulf, so I do not want our overlord in possession of the regalia. The problem is that my fellow barons and I wish to put another man into the regency, a man we can trust to hold fast to the Magna Carta principles over which we have just fought a civil war.

"If Longsword gets the true regalia that can legitimize a coronation, he may well murder Henry and supplant him. Our proposal is to boot Longsword aside and appoint Ramon of Toulouse as regent. He is an honourable man and will step aside for Edward when the boy attains his majority."

There was more, I told the silent boys. Ramon was to be given a sacred sword that is part of the regalia as token of the northern barons' utter commitment to his cause. "Also, I shall have a portable altar made, and use it to secretly transport the two most vital coronation icons. These, of course, are the Holy Roman Empress' crown and the great ruby ring that had once been the possession of the Saxon king, Alfred the Great." The boys' eyes widened.

I continued: "When he claims to have inherited these powerful icons of English monarchy, Ramon could establish as legitimate his bid to be a regent of royal blood. It's a lie, but in a good cause."

"And there is yet more," I told my grandsons. "Your father is to become a Templar knight and will stand aside from his inheritance of Bank Hall and all its lands in favour of you, Thurstan, as the elder son. I have a great deal of gold for you both and you will become lords even among your fellow barons."

Thurstan spoke first. "Grandfather: if you plan to hide the regalia here in Chester, how will you do that without the earl knowing?"

I had to shrug. "There's a monk of whom Adam of

Lonsdale speaks well, one Walter of Pinchbeck. He helped us conceal the regalia when I first, er, obtained it. Walter said he could introduce us to Abbot Hugh of Chester."

Thurstan shook his head. "Don't. We know Hugh Grylle. He says our masses and teaches us our religious lessons. He is very much the earl's man. He will talk, and will hand over everything to Earl Ranulf, grandfather. You should find another hiding place."

I tugged at my beard. "The crown and ruby…" *and sword,* I privately added, "will stay with me but I should separate them from the regalia. Is there another abbey nearby?"

This time, Robert spoke. "There is a new abbey, at Stanlaw, where we sometimes hunt. It's by the Mersey river. The abbot is said to be a very holy man."

"Very well," said Frederick, "I shall go and see him and get Walter the watchdog installed among his congregants, and then we shall perhaps have our hiding place."

Several days later, I rode out of Chester to go 'home' to Bank Hall in the Fylde, a place I had hardly seen since my boyhood. There to greet me as I rode up was the ancient stablemaster who had taught me my horsemanship so many years ago. "You look well, my lord," said the man, whose round head betrayed his origins as a descendant of the Sarmatian cavalry that once guarded Rome's misty northern border.

"And you look younger than ever on your diet of horse blood and wine, Incitatus," I responded, teasing the fellow with the name a Caesar once gave to his horse.

It was good to see the old place again. I prowled the grounds, handed out silver to the servants and gave my ailing sister Raisa a jeweled crucifix that had once graced a queen's throat. Finally I called in the reeve to account for the demesnes' running. "I'm a soldier, not a ploughman. Explain matters clearly," I demanded.

"Here, lord is a listing of the virgates and hides in each hundred," said the man, passing across a clerk's inked deed of the estate's measures and descriptions. "One virgate is enough land to support a single person, a hide will support a family. Of course the poorer the quality of the soil, the larger the measure. We have little infertile upland in the Banastre demesnes, so the size of our hides is smaller than many.

"As for taxes, we assess the food rents by the area we call a feorm, and your tenants have three major duties to you: to provide military service, fortress work and bridge repair. The king's verderers oversee the forests in Bowland."

"Do we pay for that?" I asked sharply.

"No, lord, the king does that, and allows them to take a buck and a doe each Michaelmas." Privately, I thought that the rogues probably take more than that.

The steward opted to move on, turning his master away from

what could become an uncomfortable train of thought. "In turn, lord, you are aware of your duty to the crown. For every five hides you hold, you must provide one fully-armed soldier to the king's service."

"Yes, yes, I know that," I said testily, "and I know other military matters: that every pole's length of a fortress wall needs four men to defend it. Get on with the incomes!" The steward paled, I was stifling a yawn and the drowsy afternoon looked set to become a recitation of lands and incomes, of vert and venison, rents and tithes, when a clatter in the courtyard announced an arrival.

It was my excuse. "Yes, yes," I said testily. "Just get on with matters." Outside, the dusty figure dismounting and handing the reins of his horse was Nickell of Hurcott, the weaver I had summoned from Kidreminster, cloth-making capital of England, to carry out part of my crusading scheme. The man had made good time to cross England, because he had followed the ancient Roman roads. Most forest dwellers could barely find their way home to their nameless villages if they went afield even a short distance. They lived and died in their tiny hamlets with no knowledge of the world outside.

Nickell, thanks to the cloth trade that was carried on along the roads built by the Romans, was a rare being, an experienced traveler who could successfully find his way across scores of miles. He had just completed a journey that few could manage in the England of that time.

"Nickell, over here," I greeted him, and the man whacked dust from his jerkin and hurried across the cobbles. "Your journey went well?"

"Very well, lord," said Nickell.

"And how is my old friend Sir John Biset? And his lovely sisters, Margaret and Aubrey?"

"Well, lord, and they send their greetings."

"Good." Time to end the courtesies. "I have a task for you, Master Nickell. I want you to create the winding sheet of Christ, the actual burial clothes of Our Lord."

Chapter X: Image
Frederick

Adam of Lonsdale had told me what his churchmen knew about how the body of Jesus would have been treated after it was removed from the execution post on the hill of Golgotha. "Frederick," he warned, "we do not know all this for fact, but the gospel writers have recorded some things and we know others from the practices of the day." He went on to tell me just where Christ's wounds would have been, how the body would have been washed, embalmed and linen-wrapped. It would have left marks on that shroud, a faint portrait made on the linen in the oils and unguents of the sticky, scented resin called myrrh that was used in embalming.

Then Adam told me some other facts that inspired my idea to create a sacred icon: "The ancients used myrrh as a flavouring in wine, and the evangelists tell us that Jesus was given wine with myrrh mixed into it before he was crucified. After his death, he would have been anointed with the substance, too. If you burn it, the resin has a bitter stench like the earth itself, but it does not melt. Instead, it expands a little."

Memories of the story of Veronica – her name came from

vera-icon for 'true image' – came to me. She it was who used her veil to blot the blood and sweat from the face of Jesus as he carried his cross to Golgotha. When she finished her task, the face of Christ was left imprinted on the linen.

The story resonated down the centuries and painted veils became a favoured religious icon that many pilgrims brought back from Rome and Compostela. It occurred to me that I could use the idea and have my own, confidence-inspiring holy relic to assure our troops that they had the blessing and protection of God. It was not blasphemy but a mere *ruse de guerre*, one that Lionheart would have fully approved.

I resolved to create an image of Christ on his own death-shroud, the holiest of holy relics, to carry as a banner at the head of our army. A clever artist could paint one onto linen in a mix of paints and resin, and if we heated that, it would be infused into the fabric, becoming part of it. I expected the surface could then be cleaned somehow so that no evidence of painting would survive. I asked Adam about winding sheets. "Well, they were very long, more than twice the length of a man, and more than a clothyard wide, so one would fold over to cover a corpse back and front."

All this was in my mind as I looked at Nickell, who was shuffling uncomfortably. "Keep still, man, you're not here for punishment," I said sharply. "This is about your skills. Tell me what you can do with a length of linen. How can you decorate it?"

Much of what he said passed over my head, and my eyes must have glazed, because he stopped abruptly after a long dissertation. What I do recall is talk of his abilities as a weaver and embroiderer, as a painter, illuminator and a stainer of textiles. There was talk of egg and oil mixtures, of distemper made from animal hooves and horns, walnut and linseed oils, glair of beaten egg whites and of gums, glues, tempera and size, whatever they were.

"Look, this is no painted wall hanging that I want you to create. I want an accurate painting of a man's corpse, back and front, with the marks of wounds, and a clear image of the face, all of it on a death shroud," I said impatiently. "I want the image fused into the fibres of the fabric so it does not appear to be merely painted on. I want it convincingly mysterious."

Nickell brushed at his neatly-trimmed beard. His eyes were dancing with delight. "This is a good challenge," he said thoughtfully. "Heat is the answer, and pressure. We can flash-heat the embalming oils. If we paint the image, impregnate the fabric with oils and pigments, then we could fuse it into the flax with a little pressure. I'll also need some iron and copper to act as a mordant, a fixative, to lock the image into the fabric, then I'd press the whole thing together. It could be done. Of course it would not be in colour. But," and he launched another spate of words as he talked through the problems.

"Lower your voice," I said. "This is a secret!"

He looked at me, surprised, unaware of his enthusiasm, and probably relieved that he was not there for punishment and agreed: "Of course, we do not bruit this abroad, it's probably sinful. I would paint this as a reverse image, with shade where light should be, a seeming-meaningless pattern that it is not obvious to an observer until it is pointed out. That would explain why nobody has recognized it for centuries.

"Of course I would have to heat it in a fireproof way, we don't want to burn the linen. Make me an iron box and we can bake the fabric." He paused, thinking hard. "Maybe a box would not work best," he said. "It would take a smith months to make one big enough, and there would be difficulties of keeping it completely air tight. Better make a smooth surface, probably of wood, to spread the winding sheet on after it is painted, then we can press the linen with a heated flat piece of iron to fuse the oils into it. That would work."

"Oh yes, I'd also impress the image of an appropriately-dated coin to put a marker of time on the shroud. Christ died when Rome ruled. We should obtain a coin from the emperor of the day."

I nodded in agreement. "Tiberius. I'll find one for you."

Nickell shook his head. "Two," he said. "I'll need two, one to cover each eye, as was the custom of the day, and best get Jewish coins, that would be more appropriate."

Inwardly, I was delighted. This Nickell of Hurcott could make me a miracle that could bring us a kingdom, and I soon left to find the coins he wanted while he started his skilled work. Making the linen itself was a simple task, for Lancastershire was awash in spinners and weavers, bleachers and dyers, and a purse of silver went a long way to buy access to the supplies and tools he needed. The local smith could make me a smoothing iron, he need not know its purpose.

Also, I could call on a Faeroese noblewoman, Rakul Jensdottir, an expert needlewoman and dyer who had worked on John's coronation robe and who, though opinionated, could be discreet. She had fled persecution and was in some distressed straits, so would appreciate a generous gift of gold for her work and for her silence. I sent a messenger to summon her from Chester, where she was in the service of Earl Ranulf. At the same time, I tasked my steward with obtaining or having made a portable altar that would go on campaign with me.

With some amendments, it would double as a secret portmanteau to carry the crown of the Empress, as well as the great ruby ring of King Alfred. I reasoned that few brigands would consider incurring the wrath of God by stealing or desecrating a sacred altar, and my own private reconstruction of one was for the purest of purposes and would, I was certain, be viewed favourably by the Deity. Just to be sure, I crossed myself. Then I stroked the pagan hammer of Thor that I wore under my jerkin, to be doubly safe.

My next task was to find Nickell two coins of Tiberius, which he said he would put into the image on the shroud to leave its own mark of aged authenticity, so I left him to begin his preparatory sketches and work his magic. While I was hunting down the Tiberian coins, I also had another piece of Roman currency on my mind.

It was all about the next piece of deceit, one involving the replica Sword of Tristan. I rode out from Bank Hall to nearby Waleton to consult a coiner there, a man whom I knew illicitly trimmed the king's money and melted down the clippings to make new coins. After I uncovered his forgeries, Robert Westman of Waleton had performed some useful services for me, grateful that I had not punished him for his crimes. Now I had need of his skills again.

"Westman, look at this," I handed him a gold *aureus* of the Emperor Carausius, who had ruled Britain about 300 years after the death of Christ. "I want you to put a new profile on this coin. It need not be very accurate, nobody knows what the man looked like anyway. I want you to smooth out Carausius' head, and replace it with an image something like this. Importantly, make a clear die and stamp these letters where Carausius' own name and titles once were. Leave untouched Ceres and her sheaf of corn on the other side, we want that to prove the age of the coin."

The small image of a man's profile, roughly drawn in charcoal on a scrap of lambskin that I handed to him could be anyone, and would be almost anonymous when the coin was amended, but the lettering would tell the story. It would carry the name of Tristan, also known as Drusanus of Lothian, and the altered coin would be fused into the hilt of the sword I had ordered made for Ramon of Toulouse.

The forgery would help to identify the sword as that of the ancient Britonic king – the name Tristan means 'clashing swords' – and would make the replica more credibly part of an English coronation regalia. It should be enough to deceive Ramon and his court, I felt, because he would be told of the sword's known provenance as a treasured relic. With that established, Ramon would be told: "Take this sacred sword back to the battlefield!"

Westman was examining the Roman aureus. "This is good gold, quite pure, very workable," the forger murmured. "It may be a little soft, though, in a sword hilt. What I can do is alloy the gold with one-fourth silver, and heat it in a solution rich in iron. I use brick dust. This causes the silver to leach out to the surface, and I can burnish that so it appears to be the best quality gold, but is harder. You can make some fine 'gold' coinage this way."

I shook my head. "They'll hang you one day," I said, "but

first, make this coin for me."

Chapter XI: Rules
Alaric

There was much to learn before I would be accepted as a Templar knight, and Adam of Lonsdale, that inky scholar-monk who was my father's confessor had schooled me carefully about the order. "Some of their rites and ceremonies are highly secret," he said, "and they may even harbour heretical beliefs, which is curious, as they have been the Holy Father's own elite guard almost since their inception."

I learned that they had been formed as a poverty-stricken order of military monks who lived on charity and whose purpose was to protect Christian pilgrims on their journey to the Holy Land. "They were few at the beginning, just a dozen or so French knights. They were quartered in King Baldwin of Jerusalem's palace where the old Temple of Solomon had stood, and this gave them their name," Adam explained.

The knights followed the Benedictines' rules and swore oaths of poverty – their insignia showed them riding two knights to one horse, so poor were they – and chastity and blind obedience. They also swore to follow the crusaders' vow and they adopted the Cistercians' white habit, emblazoned with a red cross. The blend of monastic obedience and military discipline attracted hordes of fervent recruits, said Adam, and the order arranged itself into four tiers of brethren: the fighting knights as heavy cavalry; the light cavalry serjeants and two tiers of non-combatants who dealt with the order's spiritual and temporal needs.

"The pope took the Templars to his bosom, blended their estates with the Church's, exempted them from taxation and tithes and gave them church privileges. This worked badly, as it caused jealousy among regular churchmen, but the order grew in wealth and power and soon had dozens of commanderies from Palestine all across Christendom," Adam had schooled me. He added that the Templars also built great castles to command the routes to the Holy Land and to control the Mohammedans in Palestine itself. Those who took the Temple's vows were noted as pious monks in the cloister, and as terrifying, disciplined warriors who were first in the battlefield, and last to leave it. Should they be defeated, they were forbidden to offer ransom and to a man when defeated had always refused to deny their faith and died unbroken, as martyrs.

All this was in my mind as I met some of those who would be my fellows: Sir John Gardiner who had fought at Acre, Guillame FitzJohn, Comte de Bosquet and the newest Templar, Jacquin de Grimshaw, a Lancashire knight who had recently devoted his life to God after some sinful years. They spelled out the religious life for me: to hear divine office at the canonical hours, to honour the calendar's monastic fasts and vigils and to venerate the Virgin Mary.

"We may not gamble or swear or drink, we live in community but are not cloistered, although novices do require permission of the Master to leave the temple grounds," Gardiner told me.

I learned that the knights alone wore the white surplice with its proud red cross, the serving brothers and serjeants wore black habits and acted as soldiers or servants. "Our role as knights is to fight," Gardiner impressed on me. "We are Christ's warriors. You will fit well with our brotherhood, you are already a warrior, now you will become a monk, too."

In truth, I was uncertain of matters. The zest had gone from my life and I had turned to the church as a simple way out. I had lost the anchor of my life when my wife Virginia died. My mother was cloistered away as an abbess, the man I had been brought up to regard as my father was dead, and the man who had arrived in my life and been revealed as my true father was a brutal professional soldier who might mean well but who had not made connection with me, although he seemed to have linked well with my sons, his grandsons, who themselves wanted only to be warriors.

Now I was about to embark on a life devoted to Christ but I felt so undecided that I had quietly secreted away a fortune in gold, breaking the vows of poverty and obedience even before

I took them. Well, I was not yet a Templar, I could still walk out of the complex and into the swarming city of London, for ever or just for a few hours, and under the curious eyes of the porters, that is what I did.

Twenty paces outside the gates, a familiar burly figure on horseback was approaching, heading a small troop of cavalry. Frederick. He reined in, halting alongside me, and leaned down to speak, but his palfrey began tonguing his bit and passaging about. Frederick growled, cuffing it casually on its neck. The horse at once stood stock-still. "And where are you going, my boy?" he asked gruffly.

I could not lie. "To clear my thinking," I said slowly.

He nodded, not without sympathy. "Couldn't be a monk, myself," he said. "Go and get rat-arsed. It's your last chance." He waved off-handedly, nudged his steed and moved on. I did not see him glance at one of his troopers, nor did I see the meaningful jerk of the head.

My mind was swirling. Could I do this, or should I tell the Templars I was too old at nearly two score of years to learn new routines? I was still deep in thought as I stepped under the low lintel of a pothouse where a green bush, the old sign of hospitality, hung above the door and an empty beer tun stood beside it. "Wine," I said, and soon I was desperately pouring down my throat the thin red stuff they served me. Several hours later, as I was swaying on my stool, I became aware of two large, dark-complected villains who were addressing me.

"You look unwell, friend," one said. "Can we help you out into the fresh air?" I was stupid with drink and shook my head, but they gently hauled me to my feet and although I could have resisted, I somehow felt it might be a good idea to get outside. They half-carried me, one each side, to the doorway, and I dimly saw a man in monk's cowled habit stand abruptly. He had been sitting quietly and alone against the wall, his hood well forward over his brow. He was working his way across the room, towards us. My new acquaintances did not notice, and now we were outside, in drizzling rain that felt so good I turned my face up and stuck out my tongue to catch the dampness.

One of my companions was fumbling at my waist cord, the other was tightly gripping my arm, now both my arms. I stumbled, trying to pull away. Even drunk, I recognized the actions of a cutpurse. I shook off the restraining hands and the fellow swore. Suddenly, he had the gleam of a blade in his fist. My own knife had been stealthily lifted from my belt. I backed to the wall, elbowing at the fellow who had re-gripped my arm, and the knifeman stepped forward to thrust at me, but even when drunk, a trained soldier can fight.

I knocked his wrist and knife upwards with my forearm and blundered against him. The danger now, I knew was from my left, where the cutpurse threatened. A movement caught my eye. The hooded man had followed us into the small courtyard and he was swinging a backhanded blow into the carotid at the side of the fellow's neck, choking the shout the thief had opened his mouth to make.

Eye-blinkingly fast, the hooded monk seized the thief's lank hair and jerked his head down, face towards the floor. With his other fist he chopped forehand, punching fiercely at the nape just as you'd kill a rabbit. This was no rabbit, but the monk was no weakling. He was a powerful, trained man administering a fearsome downward chop. It broke the cutpurse's neck and the fellow slumped silent to the mud-slimed cobbles.

The knifeman had lurched sideways as I blundered into him but he had regained his balance and, swearing, readied to stab his blade at the hooded man's unprotected side. I lashed out a foot and kicked the thief's ankle and he slipped again, half-falling into a crouch. Before he could rise, my protector turned, jerked his right knee ferociously upwards under the man's jaw and for the second time in a half minute snapped a man's neck.

The knife clattered onto the cobbles as the thief's head went sharply back at an odd angle. Then he was limp, sliding to the stones. "Come on, out of here," the hooded man hissed, grasping my arm. I probably gaped, stupidly. The voice was Frederick's. "Move!" he hissed again, and shoved me towards the exit from the small court. "Not a time to linger here, my boy. Go!" And we went.

Chapter XII: Initiation
Alaric

Frederick had sent a couple of troopers to follow me, of course, and when one reported back to him on my presence in that sordid den of a pothouse, he had elected to see for himself. "As well that I did, or you'd have had a length of steel in your ribs," he grumbled while I doused my sore head in a leather pail of cold water. "What were you thinking, going out into those sokes unarmed?" I muttered that I wasn't weaponless, I'd had a knife but the cutpurse had seized it. Frederick snorted. "Been better if you'd been unarmed altogether," he said. "not much use arming your attacker, eh?" Now it was my turn to grunt.

"Anyway," he said, "what about your initiation? Are you going forward with it?" He startled me. I'd been considering changing my mind, but when the old warrior put it so bluntly, my pride would not let me admit that.

"Of course," I said, hoping I sounded indignant. "Why not?"

"Didn't take you for a monk," he said, "but then…" his voice tailed off. "You'll be fighting, of course." He paused, "and you won't have to do the vigil, you've done that already, I suppose."

He referred to the rituals attendant on the entry into

104

knighthood, ceremonies involving sponsors, a night vigil, ritual cleansing and prayers, sermons about a knight's duties and allegiances, symbolic dress, oaths, warnings and threats of divine retribution and eternal damnation for those who backslid, and eventually the adoubement, accolade and dubbing with a blow from the flat of a sword. This was the ceremony called the colee that precedes the awarding of the knightly spurs.

It was all nominally concerned with honour and chivalry, but in truth skill in combat was of far more importance than the elaborately protective and adulatory respect for women which the code technically demanded. The Normans had long since dispensed with that, and continued to indulge their taste for rape and oppression, I thought sourly. Only might was important, for all the lip service some knights paid to fine chivalric manners. It was why the king often had to issue a writ of distraint to force the reluctant into knighthood (and his service) because many felt the rank was no longer honourable or desirable. Instead, they answered the writ by paying a fine, usually in the region of 40 pounds of silver, to be exempted from service.

Frederick was eyeing me. "Yes," I said hurriedly, "Earl Ranulf dubbed me, years ago." He stayed silent. "I still have to undergo the Templars' rituals," I said. "But nobody tells you what they are beforehand." He nodded.

"I've heard some things, " he said. "Just be obedient, suffer anything. It's a series of tests."

He was correct, and a few days later I was undergoing them. Like every Templar, I was sworn to secrecy about the rites, but later, churchmen made specific charges against our order, calling us heretics. They said we denied Christ three times, like Peter, that initiates were commanded to spit on the Holy Cross and must kiss the others of our order on the base of the spine and below the navel. They said, too, that we drank a 'cup of death' potion from a severed skull, we worshipped an idol in the form of a mummified, bearded male head recovered from the Temple Mount in Jerusalem and we claimed the true Messiah was John the Baptist, whose head it was that we adored.

My oaths mean I can neither deny nor confirm these statements, but it is true that we underwent training to simulate the kinds of torture and humiliations we might undergo should we become captives of the Saracens. By these practices we could better resist our enemies, keep our beliefs pure and go gladly to our deaths, without becoming apostates.

We learned the secret and not-so-secret history of the Order, such as the story of the battle of Montgisard, where just 500 Templar knights acted as shock troops. They rode ahead of 3,000 Christian infantry to shatter the enemy ranks and defeat Saladin's army of 26,000 Saracens. The sultan so feared the

Order that after the Crusaders' disastrous defeat at the Horns of Hattin, he bought every captive Templar and had all 230 of them executed.

That threat did not make us afraid. We were a fierce spiritual militia and we learned the blessing of St Bernard, that a Templar knight's soul is protected by the armour of faith and his body protected by the armour of steel and 'need fear neither demons nor men.' I even swore an oath that if I violated my secret vows, my skull should be sawn open and my brains dried in the sun.

For me, the worst part of the whole long initiation came when, blindfolded, I was told I would have to kill a small child. I was guided to a table and a knife put into my fist. My other hand was guided, and I felt under it the warm heartbeat under the soft skin of a living belly. My ears were full of the blood-sound of roaring and from a long way distant I heard the inquisitor urging me to strike, to kill the child. I had undergone the humiliations and fears they had forced on me, but this was too much and I came within a breath of turning away.

Then, through the din in my ears came my father's voice, calming and reassuring. "Just be obedient, suffer anything, it's a series of tests," he was saying again. My throat hurt from the gulping but I had trust in what Frederick had said. He surely would not mislead me. I blindly hammered the knife down, driving it into the helpless little belly and felt the warm gush of the blood across my hand as the child died with a muted whimper.

My gut heaved and I turned away, spitting sour vomit. To my surprise, there was a murmur of approbation from the group of men I sensed around me, and a strong arm circled my shoulders as my chest heaved. "Remove the blindfold," the inquisitor said in a kindly voice. "Alaric, you have triumphed in the last test of obedience." Someone tugged the blinding cloth clear, and I looked down, tears welling, to see that I had been tricked. The small child was no child, but a young lamb, its belly shaved, and even as I had thrust my dagger into its little chest, someone had mercifully slashed its throat. The creature had died as painlessly as could be managed and I had proved my obedience to the Order.

So, after the secret ceremonies and the swearing of grim oaths, I had the red linen cross sewn on my surplice. I vowed not to turn my back on an enemy, not to return alive from a defeat and not to bear arms against a Christian. I saw the results of the least disobedience, too: several brothers who had committed minor transgressions were ordered for the next year to eat their food from the floor of the barracks and if the dogs contested with them for their meals, they were to yield humbly and not drive the beasts away.

At length, our days of prayer and hard military training were coming to an end and we readied to move from our riverside compound and begin our journey to France.

My father Frederick arrived again at the Temple and spoke with the Master, a normally-autocratic figure who seemed curiously subservient to the old warrior, and I was summoned and told I would be accompanying Frederick on a special mission before I left for France. It turned out to be a journey to the New Forest, the royal hunting ground near Southampton where my mother Blanche was abbess of the priory at Romsey.

The Abbess Frances, as her church name was, received me warmly, Frederick less so, and sent a message for another noblewoman to join us in the stone reception chamber where visitors could meet the religious of her order. While we waited, she took us into the chapel to view a new painting of Saint Christopher she had commissioned. "To keep you both safe on your journeyings," she said with a sidelong glance at Frederick. As I examined the mural, I spotted two small figures kneeling in prayer next to the saint. My mother saw my look and smiled. "You and your father," she said. "It is a new fashion to ask the saint to watch over you, and perhaps having your likenesses next to his will remind him of the request."

The gesture was touching and I sought words of gratitude, but already Blanche was guiding us back to the reception room, where an auburn-haired woman of considerable presence was introduced to us as Elizabeth of Hale, a royal justiciar and representative of our child king, Henry of Winchester.

Frederick had briefed me before the meeting. "The justiciar is one of the Crown's highest officers," he said, "He, or she in this case, is a person empowered to act in the king's absence. It is a somewhat undefined role at the moment, as the king's authority is already delegated to a regent until Henry is old enough to rule. The justiciar's role has also been eroded since Lackland lost the crown's French holdings and the king is no longer out of England as he used to be.

"However, William Marshal, Henry of Winchester's regent, has been weaving a web of influence and he has recruited Bess of Hale as justiciar. The fact is, she has great land holdings in the north and has been battling against some repressive laws of Lackland's, notably the principle of merchet."

I nodded. I knew that merchet was a hugely unpopular tax, a marriage fee levied on widows who wanted to take a new husband. It had begun as a fee paid by a tenant to his lord for permission to marry off a daughter, but crafty King John had used it to wring fortunes from wealthy widows, often under the threat of forcing them into marriage to one of his cronies. Those Norman hangers-on almost always took over the widow's estates and fortune, disinheriting her children.

Frederick was speaking again: "Marshal wants to earn support for his boy king, and Bess of Hale may be the key to swaying the great northern barons. She and a coalition of others with fortunes wish merchet abolished, and want the heriot death duty similarly curbed. If Marshal can push through those changes, and earns her favour, he will also gain the support of those she influences."

It made sense, but I was also aware that Marshal's rival for the regency, Lackland's half-brother William Longsword would not welcome any erosion of the regent's powers. This I mentioned. Frederick understood. "Bess is here discreetly. She and your mother the abbess, who as a d'Oate has strong links to the barons of the north, are secretly in discussions with Marshal. Bess explains her presence here as merely being with her baliff on an outlaw hunt. Lawbreakers need only to escape the hundred where they are outlawed to be safe, as the constable of that region is responsible for the hue and cry, but his authority is only for his own administrative section, his own hundred.

"Bess's story is that she wants the law changed so that outlaws may be pursued across the land, not merely across one county, and she is seeking to have that change made."

It was all very well, but I did not see Frederick's part in all this, and I said so. He grinned his wolf-like grin. "Treasure, my son," he whispered. "I am giving your mother a king's ransom in gems. She can buy influence, she can even hire an army to unseat Longsword and ease the way for our man Ramon of Toulouse. We will one day have a good king, thanks to a bad king's fortune."

I paused. I could never quite keep up with the old rogue and his king-making. "Gold? Is that why the Master was so deferential to you, at the Temple?" Frederick grinned again. "No, I promised him something holy, something the very holiest," was all he would say. "Everyone," he added, "has a price. Your Master may have plenty of gold, but he does not have what I have promised, and that thing is much more valuable to him."

Chapter XIII: Monstrance
Frederick

It was plain to me that Alaric was torn by his loyalties. As a
Templar knight, he was sworn to the service of the Church,
but he also saw the unjust persecution of the saintly Ramon of
Toulouse, who was beset, in the person of the grasping, cruel
Simon de Montfort, by the same church he and Alaric both
served. That venal pope, Innocent – and what a misnomer that
name was! – had decreed that those who went on his unjust
crusade against Ramon and the so-called heretic Cathars would
not only be assured of a place in heaven, but could keep the
lands and loot they stole from the southern French.

Of course, this attracted to the cause every landless second
son, vagabond and pillage-inspired mercenary in France,
and de Montfort, with Rome blessing his slaughter of fellow
Frenchmen, headed the charge. All of this I had pointed out
to Alaric, but what finally persuaded him to endanger his soul
in the cause of upholding what was so obviously right was that
Pope Innocent had quietly abandoned the sacred principles of
Pax Dei, the Peace and Truce of God that kept feuding lords
apart, or risk damnation.

Our overlord Ranulf felt his obligations to the English

crown had weakened since John's death, and a pious man, he was deeply disturbed by the pope's actions in stepping away from the Pax Dei and in turning the plunder-hungry nobles of northern France against their cousins in the south. He had met Ramon of Toulouse and recognized his honesty and integrity, so when Ranulf declared that he would fulfill an earlier vow to go on Crusade – Egypt was the target – he was soon persuaded to halt along the way and use his forces to defeat Ramon's enemies. I said that the Templars and I would meet him there, and would continue on to North Africa with him once Toulouse had been relieved.

So, Alaric would join me in France to fight for Ramon, but first I had to visit his mother, Blanche, at Romsey, where she was the Abbess Frances. There, although she was nominally a Benedictine, she followed the austere principles of the Gilbertines and oversaw a 'double' monastery of nuns and monks. All were devoted to the religious life and to works of mercy for the lay community around them, and they supported themselves largely through the efforts of a complement of lay brothers who worked the land, most of which was in granges remote from the abbey itself.

I knew something of the religious community's disciplined daily routines and marvelled at their rigours. High Mass and seven canonical offices from Nocturnes to Compline filled the horarium of the 17-hour ecclesiastical day, and private masses sung by chantry priests at side altars kept the church bustling at all hours as they worked to benefit the souls of their congregation. For myself, my annual confession was enough, and it was a thorough and uncomfortable event I performed around Eastertide right before my yearly communion. My sparing performance of ecclesiastical duties did not impress Alaric and I was uncomfortable with the idea that Blanche, too, might question my devotion. The thoughts were uppermost in my mind as I rode up to the familiar gatehouse at Romsey and was ushered to a chamber to await the abbess and her chaperone.

Soon enough, Blanche swept in and to my surprise almost at once dismissed the young nun who had accompanied her. "Thank you, Sister Ailsa," she said peremptorily. "You may leave us now." The girl opened her mouth in protest, aware that even the abbess should not be left alone with a man. "Just close the door as you leave," said Blanche. "We shall not bar it."

She turned to me, "I have news for you, Frederick," she said in a low voice. Characteristically, she came swiftly to the business of the day. "It is news that is not for idle ears. I plan to leave this abbey." The revelation stunned me. I had imagined her settled for life, but here she was, past her 50th year, leaving a lifelong dedication to God's service.

"Your plan, madam?" I asked quietly. What she would say

interested me absolutely.

She looked at me with a calm, level gaze. "To change matters for the women of England and to make a pilgrimage. I will visit my religious sisters in France to enlist their aid in persuading the king of France to influence our king, and I shall also visit the Holy Father in Rome."

I nudged with my foot the small leather bag I had carried into the abbey. "This, then, may be of use." She took it with a skeptical look, and tugged the drawstrings open as she placed it on the table top. The glinting hoard within utterly caught her gaze, and she gasped as she poured out the contents of the bag. It was, I felt, a highly satisfactory result, but only for Blanche, who once had loved me with passion. Matters had changed, her feelings for me seemed now as cold as a hound's nostril, and I regretfully came back to the present.

Before us, on the beeswax-polished oak of the table, was a king's ransom in jewels, plus a small amount of gold in the form of Roman *aureii*. It was a sizeable fortune, but only a portion of the loot I had stolen from Lackland John. The gleaming mound of precious stones was mostly a collection that John had confiscated or forced from his hangers-on, plus several pieces which possessed ecclesiastical importance. Chief among them was an opal and pearl-studded monstrance made of gold and adorned with a sapphire the size of a plover's egg. The priceless case had built into it a small, sealed vial of

Roman glass that was half-filled with a dark liquid.

"The true Blood of Christ," I said. "Preserved by a wealthy man called Joseph of Arimathea from the Holy Land. He reputedly had Christ buried in his own tomb, and this sacred relic was held by monks in the northeast until Norsemen sacked their abbey and looted it. Three centuries later, King Richard took it as part payment of the ransom of a Norwegian princeling."

Blanche handled the precious object lovingly, and looked up at me with shining eyes. I could not resist. "Not only the Lord rewards you," I said, smugly. Her eyes narrowed, and she gave me a sharp look. I quickly retreated. "I shall tell you how to reach Isaac of Norwich and his moneylender brethren so that you can convert to gold any jewels you do not wish to keep," I said. "Then you can use the coin to do the Lord's work as you see fit."

Blanche eyed me coolly. "Let us go to the chapel," she said, "to thank Him for this." I noted my non-involvement in her gratitude and trailed along reluctantly. I had prodded at the ashes of our relationship to see if there was still a spark, or even a dull ember. There was nothing. I trailed along to the chapel, oddly relieved.

In the dim light of the church, I saw that a number of the clergy were half-sitting, half-standing at their devotions. "They are using a thing called an act of mercy," said Blanche, following my glance. "They have a small shelf on a tip-up seat – the misericord – against which they can support themselves but also remain standing during the long hours of prayer." I smiled quietly. I too had a misericorde, but it was a knife concealed at the nape of my neck. I also used it for an act of mercy: to administer the *coup de grace* to a fallen enemy. My thoughts were interrupted by Blanche's actions.

She strode to the front of the chapel, shook back the sleeves of her scapular and clapped her hands. The nuns' low susurration of prayer ceased. She spoke quietly, but her voice carried. "Today," she announced, "we have received our own miracle. We have been given the holiest of relics, drops of Our Saviour's own sacred blood. This will transform the work of our priory and we shall have to plan accordingly.

"We will at once begin a novena of prayer to thank God for this blessing and for this new opportunity and duty. Will the senior members of our community please now leave the chapel and gather in the chapter house. Please ensure that all our brethren who should be present are also in attendance. All other clergy will remain here, and begin the novena until you receive further instruction."

And so I saw Blanche begin the transformation that would make Romsey Abbey into an important place of pilgrimage. There was no part in it for me, not that I wanted it, and I could see that my small abbess no longer entertained thoughts of a life outside her religious one. She might have borne our child, but I was no longer of importance in her life. In a curious way, I felt a burden lifted from me. The responsibility I had felt since learning of our son, and that she had immured herself in an abbey, had fallen away. She had enough treasure to carry out her dual mission of presenting the miraculous blood to the faithful and of following her plan to free widows from the tyrannous tax burdens that John had imposed. Just for luck, I rubbed the small silver hammer, Thor's *mjollnir*, under my tunic. Blanche had her God, and I shared Him, but I also paid an acknowledgement to the ancient deities.

I had done my duty by the mother of our son. Now, with a clear conscience – apart from the justifiable deceits I planned - I could go to war to help fix England's king on a firm throne. Only the Pope, the King of France and the warrior earl Simon de Montfort stood in my way. Life was good and no March hare ever felt more dizzily elated.

Chapter XIV: Shroud
Alaric

My father Frederick seemed in an especially good mood as we rode to the coast to take ship for France. I knew he had seen my mother at her abbey, but I had respected her wishes not to go there, she said it would cause her too much pain. Frederick and I met at Winchester with my fellow Templars Jacquin de Grimshaw, Guillame FitzJohn, and the Crusader Sir John Gardiner, who had brought along his troubadour Francis Molens, a cherubic Yorkist whose looks had gulled many before they discovered his true nastiness in a tavern fight.

"I have some real treasures for you and your clergy, Alaric," Frederick announced. "Here is the vital symbol for Ramon, the sacred sword of Tristan." He handed me a leather-wrapped package, which I unfolded with shaking hands.

Inside was a beautifully-crafted double-edged cruciform sword with an iron wheel pommel that exactly balanced the weighty length of the gleaming blade. And what a blade! It had ghostly, swirling serpentine patterns in its mingled carbon and steel that seemed to writhe as the light caught them. The guard below the leather-wrapped hilt was brass, and was fitted with a small ring that would protect the finger the swordsman would hook over the guard as he pulled the blade free. I examined the pommel closely. Something just below it had caught my eye. Inset and fused into the hilt, cleverly crafted so both sides could be seen, was a gold coin of Roman origin.

The goddess Ceres, bringer of crop fertility was the familiar figure on one side, bringing her sheaf of wheat. On the other face of the coin was a man's profile, smoothed by use, but the die-stamped lettering around the rim of the coin was more protected and had remained legible. It bore the name 'Drusanus' and 'Lothiani,' – 'Drusus of Lothian.' It was the ancient Britonic name for Tristan and his misty northern kingdom.

I turned to Frederick excitedly. "This is not just the coronation sword, this is a proven legend!"

He was looking at me with a curious gleam in his eye, a look that made me slightly uncomfortable. He must have caught my hesitation, for he suddenly boomed out: "Of course, my boy, of course! That is a coin of Roman age, with the king's own name on it. It can be nothing other than the true blade of Tristan, whose very name means 'clashing swords!'"

Once again, I examined the wondrous sword. "I can almost feel its power, its sacred soul. To think this was once handled for God by the greatest Christian warrior! This holy relic will empower the arm of Ramon and will show his troops how the Lord is with him in his righteous battles." I paused, and

Frederick interspersed: "It is time. It is time for this sacred sword to go back to the field of battle and to lead the Lord's troops to victory."

The others gathered around to view the miraculous blade and I caught Gardiner glancing quizzically at Frederick. "How did you come by this icon?" he asked softly.

"Oh, Lackland had it stowed away with the other coronation regalia," my father answered quickly. "He was a magpie who coveted and hoarded treasures." Gardiner was running a finger along the blade's edges.

"It is a miracle surely," he said, "that this is as smooth and true as the day it was forged."

Frederick's head came up sharply. "Forged? Oh, yes, by the bladesmith. Well, the king liked to keep everything looking perfect and I expect he must have had any notches and chips ground out, as the blade was kept sharp. Yes, it does seem to me to be a little worn down from its original width." Later, much later, I would recall that innocent-sounding conversation, but that day at Winchester I was so overawed by the Sword of Tristan I could hardly question anything.

And then Frederick produced his next miracle. At his signal, a man at arms reverently carried in a large, flattish leather bag that was folded over itself. Frederick gestured at the table and the man laid out the bag, opening the folds and untying the leather thongs that closed it. Frederick waved him away and by himself gently, carefully drew out a folded linen which he spread on the table top. It was far too long for the table, so he gestured again and the man at arms took one end of the linen, and moved backwards, to expose the entire thing.

I squinted but could not make out what I was viewing. It was dark-patterned in an irregular way, it was not painted, but the image was somehow burned into the herringbone weave of the fabric. The linen was at least twice the length of a man and was more than a clothyard wide. A faint, bitter, slightly resinous odour emanated from it, vaguely familiar to me. It reminded me somehow of the Holy Land, or somewhere hot and dry. Later, I would learn it was the scent of myrrh, a perfume used in embalming. Frederick was looking around, obviously triumphant.

"What are we seeing?" FitzJohn broke the silence.

Frederick gestured to one end of the dark patterning. "This, my Templar friends, is the face of Christ Himself. The image is reversed. What was light is dark, look at it thus and you will see."

It was as if scales had fallen from my eyes. I was seeing a bearded face with longish hair parted centrally, eyes closed. Below was the rest of the image: a man's naked body, hands crossed, some obvious large, diamond-shaped water stains or scorch marks marring the whole thing. As my brain took in the reverse image, I saw that the whole body was duplicated on the upper length, only this was the back of the body, imprinted on its burial cloth. There were bloodstains and slash marks, dozens of them, and I recalled that Christ was scourged before He was crucified.

Stains – light in the reversed image – at the head, wrists and feet were presumably blood marks and when I leaned in closer to examine the face, I saw that the eyes had been covered with two small coins, which I later found were probably Jewish *lepta* minted during the reign of Tiberius. It was also discernible that the face was slightly asymmetric, as if one cheek were swollen from a blow. My mind was reeling as if I had received a similar blow.

Turning to Frederick, I hardly dared to ask him: "How did you find this treasure?"

He shrugged. "It was once in the possession of the Byzantine rulers of Constantinople. When the Fourth Crusade arrived at that city a few years ago, it would have been 1203, they attacked and plundered the place. They certainly entered the Boucoleon Palace where this shroud was stored. Who obtained it, or how it was taken, I do not know but the relic was long ago lost to the Byzantines, probably at the fall of Jerusalem. It greatly angered Pope Innocent that the Crusaders should so treat fellow Christians, heretics though they were, so I suppose whoever took possession of the shroud was unwilling to take it to Rome and be excommunicated for looting. So, it has remained hidden for the past dozen years or so.

"It came to me by secret means and for no reward. The donor simply wanted it to be the inspiration of a movement to make fast the throne of England. If we can use it to save Ramon of Toulouse, it will have done that duty, and it will be installed in the cathedral at Canterbury."

There was a clatter behind me, and I turned to see that the Templars, exalted at merely being close to such a holy relic, had all fallen to their knees to pray. I joined them, and even Frederick lowered himself to the flagstones and bowed his head although I never heard him mutter any prayers.

When we were done and the shroud had been reverently re-wrapped and returned to its carrying case, Frederick announced that the Temple Master would take charge of the shroud, and would accompany us with it to France. He gestured me aside and spoke softly. "You have the sword to give to Ramon as a sign of our good faith, we have the shroud to carry before our army. Now I want you, and you alone, to view something else." He led me to his small chamber off the Great Hall and overlooking the inner courtyard at the heart of Winchester Castle. "This," he said, gesturing, "is going on our holy mission with us."

He was showing me a small, portable altar, beautifully crafted and handsomely gilded. I was impressed and somewhat surprised. My father was not a religious man – I knew of the secret pagan symbol he wore around his neck – so why he would feel he needed a place for his devotions while on campaign was a new insight for me, and I said so. He shook his head. "Sometimes, Alaric, you are a priest-taught fool. Look at this."

Frederick turned the little altar around so we viewed its back. He reached under the marble *mensa* of its tabletop, which contained, he said, the girdle of St Winefride, whose shrine was within our clan's ancient Welsh holding at Prestatyn, and pulled at an ornamental moulding.

A small panel that must have been weighted slid open, and Frederick reached into the cleverly-concealed compartment behind it to extract a velvet bag and a smallish, flat wooden case. The bag contained the vast ruby Ring of Unity; the linden wood case held the foldable imperial crown that had graced the head of the Holy Roman Empress Matilda at her coronation in Rome a century ago. "A clever one, that Maud," Frederick said approvingly. "She had the crown made so it could travel easily, see these hinged sections?" I did, and I had seen them before, but Frederick was always proud to show off the treasures that had once been under his care as King John's Jewel Master.

I was more impressed at how cleverly my father had chosen to transport the two most vital items for an English coronation. All men would understand why a soldier would take an altar on campaign, and would protect it, few would dare to tamper with such a sacred object, and almost none would suspect it was a hiding place for treasure other than an untouchable relic. The altar and its precious cargo could not be safer: it would be under Frederick's eye and only he and I knew of its secret. Or so I hoped.

Chapter XV: Claresta
Frederick

Once, I might have felt guilty at deceiving my son, but King Richard had long since taught me that a *ruse de guerre* was a legitimate deception, and to give Alaric and his fellow warrior-monks a source of inspiration, even if it was just a painted image on a length of linen, could be construed as a noble thing. "If they die in battle protecting it and their faith, they'll gain credit with God," I thought. "He might not be so understanding with me, but I'll make sure I find a confessor before I die, and that should tidy up matters."

We had been drinking thin beer, Alaric was relaxed, and the ale made him incautious, so that he leaned to me and murmured: "Father, we have the sword for Ramon, and the shroud for our troops. You sent gold for the Templars but you have said nothing about the coronation regalia. Did you hide it at Stanlaw Abbey yet?"

I had been expecting some such question, and in fact I had ridden out to the new abbey on the bank of the River Mersey a month before and convinced the prior to cooperate for the glory of God and the benefit of the realm. The churchman, impressed by the solemnity of the vow he had to make, agreed to seal a pair of heavy saddlebags and one long leather-wrapped bundle into a pier at the intersection of two barrel vaults off the abbey transept. The stonework was opened secretly by a mason I took with me, the bags of treasure and the real Sword of Tristan inserted, and the disturbed masonry re-cemented with minimal disturbance and with no witnesses but myself, two troopers and the workman. Even the prior did not know what was in the bags and I convinced him that he should make no effort to find out. I put out a story that the bags contained religious relics we were hiding from the French and with a gift of gold and the threat of God's wrath sealed the lips of the mason and the troopers.

Then I rode back to Chester and spoke with Abbot Hugh. "In the coming months you may be approached by a noblewoman who will endow and install a stained glass window in your abbey. Your duty is to cooperate with her." As the servant of my own liege lord Earl Ranulf, now away on the Fifth Crusade, Hugh was eager to oblige, and I considered again the noblewoman who would visit him.

Lady Claresta of York was an intelligent woman of many facets and she possessed a generous heart. She hunted, and in her household she kept a hunter and falconer – Joffe of Hanne – whose poacher's neck she had saved from being stretched on the gallows tree because he had once led her to a sounder of wild boar. Together they had killed three of the

129

herd, and Lady Claresta happily remembered the savage joy of that day, so when the white-bearded old falconer came to her for sustenance, she took him into her household from pity and perhaps in hopes of revisiting the thrill of the hunt.

From soft-heartedness, too, she continued to employ a blind kitchener called Pritchard whose minimal skills caused even the hall dogs to refuse his offerings. One evening, two drunken soldiers plunged him headfirst into a vat of his own boiling turnip soup, causing him considerable discomfort and the noblewoman to be cautious in future of the opportunities she offered her charity cases.

She was more optimistic about a young orphan girl who proved to have skills as an archer so good she was later refused entry to the annual competition at Nottingham Fair. "One day, you will be the king's own archer," Claresta comforted the girl, "and the name Peyton of Marrone will be famous throughout England."

Claresta herself was renowned as a wealthy heiress, daughter of a northern justiciar much favoured by King Richard and she followed a craft that few understood. She was an expert artist in stained glass.

I had met her when she was a teenage girl at the king's lodge in Oxford. I was Lionheart's companion in arms and she had impressed me with an unusual skill. She was studying the art of glassmaking. "I want to create a great coloured glass window

for a cathedral," she told me. "It will be a poem piece of colour and vibrancy, a glowing translucent gem of glass that tells a story to the faithful and glorifies God and our world."

The years had passed, we had met again at her demesne at Selby, near York, and by then she had learned her craft from a follower of the German monk Theophilus, who taught his apprentices how to use beech wood, sand and fire to create glowing glass beauty. "Beech forms an alkali that breaks the bonds of molten sand so we can work it," she explained, "You use the furnace to frit, that is to fuse but not melt the glass for a night and a day to expel the air bubbles that would form if you allowed it."

She understood that I had hidden some religious relics and I gave her details of the window I wanted made to tell a future generation of their place of concealment. She accepted both the commission and a generous purse of gold to carry out what would be a long and difficult task. As we spoke of the design she would create, she showed me her partitioned, chamber-sized furnace of stone and clay where she made such brilliant glass. The miracle was a fusion of molten sand and beechwood ash plus colouring oxides made from powdered metal. The mixture was brought together in huge heat over the course of many hours, then spread to cool without cracking in a purpose-built annealing chamber.

Claresta told me the workings of her craft. "Some colours

are attained without additives like copper, which can give you reds or greens, or powder of cobalt, for blues," she explained. "If you see the glass in the pots is changing without such additives, heat it for three hours and it will become a light saffron yellow colour. Heat it twice as long and it will take on a red hue. Some sand, rich in iron, produces glass that is coloured blue or even olive green."

To make flat glass suitable for a window piece, Claresta and her glassblowers used an iron blowpipe. They would dip and twist the end of the pipe into the vat of molten glass to snare a large blob, then blow air down the tube to expand it into a balloon of glass, taking care to remove the blowpipe between puffs in case they should inadvertently suck in a breath of flames or superheated, scorching air.

The glassblower would also swing or spin the balloon to make the piece larger and thinner. This simultaneously formed a cylinder, which the glassmaker then slit open to be flattened.

"Sometimes, instead of making coloured glass with an additive, I apply paint onto clear glass," Claresta explained. "This lets me work the colour into denser or lighter hues. For example, I might paint the whole pane piece with yellow paint, then overpaint it with red and use a pumice stone to remove parts of the top layer to give the colour greater or lesser depth in certain parts.

"Other times, I might paint with brushes made from the tails

of squirrels or badgers or donkey manes to put down a base layer of dark paint which I remove in places to create saints' faces or the folds of their robes. For that paint, I like to use crushed glass and copper mixed with wine or mild acid. When the painting is complete, I fire the whole thing in a kiln to affix the colour firmly to the glass."

The preparation of the stained glass had to be meticulous, she explained. The whole design of the window should first be drafted life-sized onto a board before it was transferred, a section at a time, onto glass. This in turn was cut with hot iron tools, sometimes sprinkled with droplets of water to encourage the breaks. The original board acted as the pattern to assemble the glass sections, which were edged and joined together with malleable thin strips of lead.

"I want my lead to be as thin as possible," Claresta said, "because I want as much light to pour through the glass as I can achieve, and not have it blocked by solid lines. I love that the French have led us away from those round, muscular Roman arches and into the slender, pointed ones of St Denys that allow us more glorious glass."

She glanced at me. "Is it a sin of indulgence? Bernard of Clairvaux said these windows were inspired by vanity, but my master mason says they are praise to God. I like to think that is more true." I had no response.

In her workshops Claresta employed specialist painters who

created the images, and skilled craftsmen whose focus was only on glass making. "My apprentices start young," she said, affectionately cuffing the head of a small boy as he passed. "You, Johannes of Thornton, what will you be?" she called out.

The child stood proudly. "One day, lady, I shall be a famous glassmaker," he said, "and I shall teach my sons and grandsons all of my skills and they will be proud of me."

Claresta laughed. "Just be sure your long nose doesn't get caught in the kiln," she said. Had she but known it, John Thornton's descendant would also be a stained glass artist, and he would use his long nose as a sly motif in beautiful cathedral windows at which people centuries later would still smile.

Chapter XVI: Refectory
Frederick

Talented Claresta supported the northern barons who were so uneasy about the regency of the boy-king, Henry of Winchester, and she may hold the key to unlocking my great secret after we are all dead. I had discussed the matter with Adam of Lonsdale, telling him: "We do not trust Longsword to honour his oaths, and we have to fix Henry firmly on the throne. The barons have agreed to support Ramon of Toulouse if he will be regent and I have hidden the regalia we will need to make Henry's coronation legitimate.

"There is a problem. Only five people know where the regalia, which includes the true Sword of Tristan is hidden, two of us are off to war and possible death while you, the third, are no longer a young man." Adam shrugged in apology. I grinned at him. "Happily, my two grandsons also have the knowledge, so, although we have to keep the regalia safe for at least a dozen years until Henry is old enough to take over from Ramon, they can be keepers of the secret.

"I am reluctant to share the hiding place with anyone else in case they usurp the throne but it is dangerous to leave such a vital knowledge in the hands of so few. I think we should reveal the secret in full sight and if needed, leave its discovery in God's hands. Can we trust Claresta with the secret? Can we safely make her the sixth person to know? If I ask her to make a window to tell the tale, we can hardly expect her not to solve the puzzle of what the window says. If we can trust her, we will in time let the world know where the regalia lies, and even if we are all six dead and gone, it will one day, God willing, be found and used."

Adam, ever the diplomatic churchman, smiled gently. "I think the lady will be as trustworthy as anyone you can find." he said. "Rest on the decision, we have more pressing needs. Stop fretting about Lady Claresta. God's will is usually done, let us now check the equipment you will need to do it." He referred to my armour and weaponry, which he had listed, and to the personal items I would need on our expedition. Ever thorough, my confessor monk who had once been a soldier, and who still wore a keen-edged blade strapped discreetly hidden on his left forearm, had studied arms and equipment.

In his readings, he had learned that the celebrated Roman infantry enjoyed some advantages over our own modern soldiery, and he had persuaded me to adopt a few of the ancients' ideas. One which impressed me was the nail pattern on the soles of Roman marching boots. The boots themselves were closed and ankle-high, but the nails that studded the soles were formed in a curving pattern. "This spreads the load diagonally as the foot strikes the ground," Adam had explained. "It makes a considerable difference to the impact of every footfall and is much less fatiguing on the march."

It was typical of the man, scholar and warrior that he was. He had noted the S-pattern of the legionaries' boot soles on a memorial stone and had wondered at the detail. Finally, he had carried out his own experiments, nailing boots in a similar pattern and had discovered its efficiency. When the time came, he had used the secret on the boots of our own soldiers and given us a marching advantage.

Adam studied other aspects of the great legions and adopted some of them, too. He told me of the Romans' legendary ability to cover long distances and still be in condition to fight. "They were reorganized by the Emperor Marius, who believed that pack mules and wagons were inefficient and slowed the legions. He saw to it that each legionary carried nearly half his own weight in armour and equipment, but could still force-march 40 miles in a day. They portered their packs on a short pole over the shoulder, as it's less tiring. No wonder they called them Marius' Mules. It's also recorded that the Caesar Gaius Julius once marched his men 100 miles in 24 hours, admittedly without their full packs, but with all their weapons. It is a tribute to them and their organization that they were still in condition to fight and win a battle at the end of that."

This practical use of reading intrigued me. "How did they

feed their troops on the march?" I wanted to know.

"Each man carried a two-week supply of food like smoked or salted meat and fish, twice-baked barley bread, dried fruit salt, and fish-paste flavouring, so they could eat from their own supplies. Usually they were given a hearty meal in the morning, and commissary wagons would travel ahead to have food available at the halts on the march."

I grunted. I envied the Romans their discipline. Too often, simply moving a modern army was a jumbled chaos of soldiery and hangers-on. It would take a considerable feat of organization to send supply wagons ahead of an advance, not to mention the danger of them being intercepted by enemy forces. It wasn't practical. I turned my attention back to the present, as Adam was waving a hand at the assembled equipment I'd need.

"Which helmet?" he asked, indicating several. I settled for two, one with a curved face plate and a newer-fashioned broad-brimmed kettle helmet which offered excellent visibility and better ventilation. There was a sword belt and patterned leather scabbard holding my wicked, long Bloodblade; and a long dagger for my belt. As always, I was already wearing a punching dagger, hidden in a lubricated scabbard at the nape of my neck.

In the array of weapons and protection before me, to complement the sword and spear was an axe with a crescent blade, and a mace, cruelly flanged, that could bite through armour.

My flat topped, curved, long shield of elmwood and leather had two straps, one to loop around the arm, the other that circled my neck so I could use both hands when fighting. It was emblazoned with the Cross of Malta that was the Banastre coat of arms, as was the gonfanon banner that adorned the shaft of my spear. The surcoat that covered my armour was white, and carried the red cross of the Crusader. This was a colour change. In earlier years, the English crusaders wore a white cross on a red ground. Now we had adopted the French red cross on white, a concession to unity that became the insignia of most nations.

Adam indicated a sleeveless leather vest with metal plates sewn into it. "Your body armour," he said. Worn over a padded canvas jacket, the vest was thigh-length, and buckled down the spine. It afforded protection as good as chain mail without its weight. I also had mail leggings which strapped in place to cover my lower limbs and groin.

Calf-length ox-hide leather boots that laced down the front; spurs, leather gauntlets and a linen shirt worn next to the skin completed my battle dress. More everyday items were on Adam's list: braided wool socks with stirrups; linen braies, or under-drawers; a large-brimmed, low-crowned hat for travelling; rosary beads (I quietly touched my hidden Thor amulet); a pitch-covered leather water bottle; dice and cup; a leather box containing thread and needles, flint, steel and tinder; wooden spoon, bowl and cup plus sheathed knife for cutting food; purse and scrip bag and a semi-circular, heavy wool cloak with hood.

This last was far superior to the cloaks of red Irish cloth worn by working men. It was military quality, fashioned after the old Roman oiled-wool *sagum*, and acted as blanket, groundsheet, coat, and sometimes, for the unfortunate, as shroud. It kept out the rain, retained warmth when wet and was probably a soldier's best friend, after his weapons. I had ordered a large quantity of them made at the weaving sheds near Winchester that had once been the Romans' imperial mills. How much more did we owe to those ancients, I wondered?

One of those debts, a fine stone-built road, was under my warhorse Sinner's hoofs as we rode south from Selby. A trained battle mount, the big black Frisian was an uncomfortable ride, but I had lost my smooth-pacing palfrey to the bloating disease and had been unable to replace him at short notice. We clopped along the arrow-straight road the empire-building Latins had constructed to link their northernmost border walls of Hadrian and Antoninus with their cities of York, Lincoln and London. The regular and smooth stones of the great north road and the King's Peace that protected it made for swift travel, and we left it regretfully for the equally swift, more ancient road of the Fosse. This ridgeway road runs south and west from Lincoln to Exeter. We followed it to the noble city of Bath and turned aside towards the sea that leads to France.

The journey took a week and we arrived near the coast at Romsey Abbey on a Friday, which did not bode well for our dinner that night, as Fridays were fasting days. I was disappointed to find that Blanche, or Abbess Frances, which is the name she took with her clerical vows, was absent with the almoner on priory business, and Adam, who had helped me control my hair so I would look my best for her, cast me a wry look. The black-cowled monks who welcomed our party seemed to miss the glance as well as my heightened colour, and we joined them for their evening meal.

It was an eye-opening experience. First, my eyes took in the stock of silver vessels, many of them gilded, the silver candlesticks and spoons; the chargers, platters, dishes and saucers of pewter that were piled up in readiness. The upper table sported a central *nef* of silver, a boat-shaped container to hold utensils, spices and a flagon of wine, and the whole board was covered in clean linen. Even the tables of the more humble each bore a large platter of precious spices. Then there was the food. I knew that as a spiritual exercise of self-restraint for about one-third of the year the Church forbade the consumption of the flesh of four-footed animals or even of animal products like eggs, milk, cheese and butter. The wily monks seemed, however, to have found many legalistic loopholes and other ways to circumvent the sumptuary laws and their dietary commandments.

Offal, bacon or other processed meat was adjudged by the abbot to be exempt from the rule and fish – it was usually cod, pike or herring – was not restricted, which opened the door to eating marine animals, so we found ourselves facing a feast that included beaver tails, conger, puffin breasts, oysters and roast barnacle goose.

"We have even eaten whale," one elderly monk confided when I asked him about the dietary restrictions. "It is allowed." I knew that noblemen would eat non-meat meals, using fake eggs made of fish roe flavoured with almonds and that they would use similar cuisine trickery to serve faux ham or venison during fast days, but I was taken aback that the religious would circumvent the sumptuary edicts. This I cautiously said to the monk who sat by me.

He trotted out what was obviously a rehearsed line of reasoning. "The sick are exempt from fasting," he said earnestly, "so they may partake of meat at all times, but generally the restrictions only apply to the refectory where we normally take our meals. If we eat elsewhere, the restrictions do not apply."

I glanced at Adam, who was listening keenly and he blinked

a warning to me. "The digestive tracts of nobles and senior churchmen are more delicate than those of common men, lord," he said carefully. "Mother Church knows this and exempts many from what might be harmful to them. It is why we first eat food that digests quickly and opens our stomachs. Should we consume heavier foods first, they would block the entrails and bring bad humours into the digestive tract."

The old monk, I noticed, ate a ginger confection first, to pave the way and 'open the stomach.' This he followed with fruit before moving onto a wooden bowl of eel broth and lastly, the 'fish' courses, when he took some oysters, beaver tails and goose.

All of these courses were served communally, the dishes being placed on trestle tables, then spooned into wood or pewter bowls or even into trenchers made from hollowed-out bread. Most diners carved bread or selected pieces of food for the plates of their table companions, but I saw that the junior servants and common people ate their meals straight off the bare planks of the table. Some people brought their own knife so they could cut off a piece of meat or fish or spear something from the stewpots, and the lower orders especially shared the drinking horns just as they shared their knives.

Adam and I sat at the linen-covered Great Table with the sub-prior and some senior monks, all of whom had their own pewter dishes. The sub-prior sipped watered wine from a fine

Roman glass decorated with a hunting scene, but the ordinary monks drank small beer. The sub-prior noted my scanning looks and said smoothly: "We follow the Rule of St Benedict, lord, who said that we should live plainly. We restrict ourselves to a small flagon of wine each day, but the good saint did not place a restriction on the amount of beer." In fact, on 'normal' non-fasting days, most monks drank about a gallon of beer and were allowed five or six eggs, a loaf of bread weighing two pounds and two pounds of fish or meat. It was more than twice the intake of a peasant doing heavy work.

"No wonder they're all fat," I muttered to Adam as the sub-prior droned on about the austerity and demanding dictates of Benedictine rule.

It was the next night, when we ate meat in a repast that made me inwardly gasp at the affluence and direction of the abbey. Its byres and sties, fish house and curing furnace, granaries, mills, storehouses and kitchens all played a part. The kitchens were manned by a hurrying legion of bakers, cooks, sauciers, butchers, larderers, scullions, carvers and squires. Their duties were to serve several hundred clergy two large meals each day. One way this was accomplished was through the use of a stepped buffet, where dishes were displayed on a series of shelves. Servants selected, carved and delivered meals from them to the distinguished diners at the top table who cut their meats then delicately ate them with their fingers. Lesser mortals helped themselves, hacking off great smoking lumps of meat before eating them from the knife point.

In the smoky hall's centre was an open fireplace where food preparers roasted fowl, beef, mutton, pork and venison on spits that ranged from small enough for a single bird to large enough for an ox. The red-faced, perspiring cooks carefully collected all drippings to baste the meat, or to use in sauces. Ovens adjoined the fireplace, and in them bakers made pies in a huff paste of suet, flour and hot water. This stiff coffyn was almost inedible, and was simply a container for the stew within. Poorer magnates would serve the coffyn, which soaked up meat juices, to the servants.

"We do not dine so well every night," the sub-prior assured me, "but this is a feast day and the cooks have made an extra effort." And so they had. To start the feast, the kitcheners carried in a great pie, more than a clothyard wide, filled with venison that had been salted overnight, then cooked under its pastry with roast hare and a loin of veal.

Next, and to loud acclaim and calls of 'Praise the Lord!' a whole roast wild boar was carried in; roast chickens covered in a plum sauce followed, then a dozen large pies filled with the flesh of a whole roe deer, plus the meat of goslings, chickens and rabbits; all were brought in by a procession of servants. Two dozen hard-boiled eggs flavoured with cloves and saffron made a sort of stuffing for each pie. While all this was being delivered to table, a whole stag was being turned on the largest spit of the hall's fireplace. It was larded and roasted to crispness, then quartered, doused in pepper sauce and served to the diners.

More courses kept coming from the kitchens' copper vats: a sturgeon cooked in parsley, loins of crisply-roasted pork, stuffed capons, boiled ox meat from the supply that was kept salted as basic rations. Roast kid, two roast herons and dishes of jugged hare also crowded the buffet shelves.

Several hours after the feast began, pages brought in the finishing courses: jellies, cream cheese, strawberries, plums stewed in rosewater, some sweet pastries and an assortment of pears, apples, nuts and cheese. Much of it was wasted. A good number of the monks, overcome by the huge meal they had washed down with floods of cinnamon and juniper-spiced beer, were slumped, head on folded arms, asleep at the tables. I scraped back my bench, muttered my thanks to the drowsy sub-prior, whose head was nodding rhythmically, and fled the refectory.

Those who had promised to live by the Benedictine Rule needed to be reminded of their oath, I felt, for their communities were in sad need of overhaul. If we were going to France to risk our lives for religion, this was not the example we needed to see. At least, after witnessing the sumptuous lives these clerics lived, I felt better about the faked Shroud and sword. These monk-cowled gluttons were in no position to judge my actions; their sins were far worse than mine. I was merely cheating to inspire the troops. They on the other hand were indulging themselves and living off the land's fat. They *were* the land's fat, I snorted. The next morning, I left quickly, without breaking my fast. On campaign, it was usual to be hungry and I should accustom myself to it, again.

Chapter XVII: France
Frederick

So I was feeling cheerfully virtuous as we rode through the familiar wooded copses and fertile cornfields and across the saltmarshes in the hinterland of Bosham, the tidal inlet south of Winchester that was our port of departure for France. I had sailed from here for Boulogne when I went to join Lionheart on crusade, and the sight of the windmills along the low-lying coastline brought back sharp memories.

On my previous departure, the inlet and the Bosham Stream had been choked with a forest of masts and rigging of the 200 or more ships of the crusaders, and the small town had bustled with the provisioners, carpenters, smiths, shipwrights, sailors, soldiery and the omnipresent train of whores, hangers-on, thieves, holy relic-sellers, runaways and hedge-preachers that always follows an army. This time, apart from the local fishing fleet, only a dozen or so wide-beamed trading vessels lay at the wharfs, and on one of those we would make our passage across the strait the French called The Sleeve and the English called The Channel.

We handed over our mounts to the care of several stable hands at a tavern which carried a painted sign announcing the place as the 'Journey to Jerusalem' and spent a rare idle afternoon sitting in the sunlight, drinking thin ale and swapping stories with a jolly group of vicarious pilgrims, men who for pay had undertaken to go on pilgrimage for the benefit of others' souls. One told me he had made the journey to Compostela four times already and gave me useful advice about routes and hazards. Our talk ended and I thanked him with a pot of beer, which he accepted, then offered me one in return. "There's good money to be had as a professional pilgrim," he assured me cheerfully, adding with a wink: "and even better money for the holy relics you can bring back." Or take with you, I thought with a guilty twinge, then pushed the thought away. I had plenty of other things to consider, we were leaving England shortly.

Our seigneur, Ranulf de Blondeville, sixth Earl of Chester, was already in France with the troops and had agreed to divert en route to Egypt to relieve Ramon, at Toulouse, which was under siege. The four fighting friars, the Templars John Gardiner, Guillaume FitzJohn, Jacquin de Grimshaw and my son Alaric were travelling there with Adam and me to join the crusade. As escort, if we needed one, we were accompanied by a small troop of my horse soldiers. Also in our troop was the troubador Francis Molens, who had asked to join us, as did a few evil-looking Hun mercenaries who sought a ship to France, or so the innkeeper told us.

I looked hard at the Huns, stocky, weathered little men with elongated skulls that had been deliberately misshapen in childhood by being bound with flat boards. All had scarred faces from the self-inflicted slash wounds they make to mourn the deaths of their comrades or chieftains.

"They do it so they appear to weep blood, not salt tears," said Adam, who could never resist airing his knowledge.

"And they deform their heads to make themselves look fearsome," I rejoined. Adam, who had opened his mouth to speak further, looked nettled. He had obviously been about to inform me more of the blindingly obvious.

"They are fierce archers," he said, seeking the upper hand.

"Yes, they make their bows from bone, sinew and wood and they are powerful enough to kill at 200 paces," I riposted, holding up my hand to silence him. It did not work.

"And they use arrowheads of bone or horn." I turned away to end the contest. It's difficult to stop an erudite monk in full flow.

One of the Huns approached on horseback and I viewed him with interest. His eyes were slanted and deep set, his nose was unusually flat, his hair reached his shoulders and he sported a beard as thin as that of a callow youth. He wore baggy deerhide leggings, a linen tunic and leather jerkin and soft boots suitable for a horseman but that would disintegrate in a day's wet marching.

On his head he wore a pointed felt cap. Slung at his saddle bow, for he was mounted on a shaggy little pony with a long head and wide hoofs, was a conical leather helmet and a bundle that later revealed itself as body armour of bone plaques sewn onto hardened leather. A coil of rope also hung from the saddle. This was a lasso that the Huns used them to rope an enemy from his shield wall and drag him to be slaughtered.

The gold that ornamented this Hun's sword hilt, bow stave and horse's trappings marked him as an elite warrior or chieftain, and he had some knowledge of other tongues than his own. He spoke in rough French and used some Germanic terms, but the meaning was clear. He wanted employment on the campaign in France and sought to travel with us to the rendezvous. The man was unprepossessing, but had about him a focused, still presence that was more than menace. He was a *khan*, the innkeeper said, a minor king and he carried authority with him. He made his request politely, and we quickly agreed to transport his men and their mounts, and at first light we were slipping out of the Bosham inlet, carried south by the ebbing tide and the light offshore winds.

We were taking the imitation Sword of Tristan, symbol of the English nobles' genuine support, to Ramon of Toulouse to persuade him to be regent for our child king. Although we were going to war in France, our mission as Crusaders was in northern Africa. We had no intention of serving the new Pope in the French campaign against Ramon's people, the Cathars Pope Innocent had so feared that he demonized them as heretics and ordered them destroyed.

We were allies of the heretics partly to earn Ramon's regency, partly to set back the French. Instead of fighting for Rome, we sailed to defeat the papal puppet Simon de Montfort, who was captain-general of her forces against Ramon. When that conflict was done, we would continue to Egypt to join our own overlord, Earl Ranulf of Chester, on the Fifth Crusade. We should have the Church's blessing for at least half of our mission, we joked. Maybe it would cancel out the condemnation we'd receive when the Pope uncovered our perfidy.

The first phase of our journey went well, we passed peaceably through Normandy, a possession we had lost a dozen years before, and we rode unhindered into Burgundy alongside the tranquil rivers Yonne and Cure to the pilgrim town of Vezelay. On the river bank, peasants were cleaning fish – mostly pike, Alaric told me, for he was more of a countryman than I had ever been – and splitting wood to fuel the fires that would smoke their catch. It was a peaceful, pleasant and rural vista. Once inside the town walls, the scene changed to one of bustling activity. The settlement dominated by the hilltop abbey of the Benedictines is a major attraction for pilgrims, as the bones of Mary Magdalene lie there, and many of those who make the long and gruelling journey across the Pyrenees to the shrine of Santiago de Compostela begin their pilgrimage from the abbey steps.

The great Saint Bernard of Clairvaux had preached the Second Crusade here a half century before and I myself had left from Vezelay to accompany Lionheart and Philip of France on the Kings' Crusade of 1191, an age ago when I was young. Then, the town had been jammed with crusaders and their legions of followers and hangers-on, from butchers and bakers to whores, horse thieves, tricksters and runaways.

The place was less crowded now, even on market day, as it was when we rode in, but the place still thronged with shepherds and sutlers, washerwomen and wagoneers, tailors and traders and the usual flotsam of cutpurses, thieves and sellers of fake religious relics. We moved aside to avoid three lepers in their obligatory grey coats and red caps; a Jew similarly stigmatized by law wore a yellow circle on his breast and he earned our disapproving looks, but God forgive us, we all smiled at a pretty whore in her tell-tale red skirt. One of my troopers called that he'd see her at dusk, earning a growl from his serjeant.

This time, unlike my previous visit, we were able to continue on our way after staying only a day or two, because there was no dainty French king to delay matters with his jealous wrangling and timid cautions about crusading. Adam of

Lonsdale had been with me on that previous visit and he snorted with laughter as we recalled those days over some flasks of good Burgundy wine in an auberge.

"We wasted weeks here because of that pansy Philip," Adam snorted. "He was like a girl who could never make up her mind, he was simpering and timid and jealous of Richard's power and skills. Philip was no kind of man, not like Lionheart. Richard hunted wild boar, Philip went hawking for sparrows," he said. "Just a glance at their standards told it all. Lionheart had leopards on his gonfanon, the King of France had lilies on his."

Unfortunately, Adam had grown somewhat deaf as he aged and he spoke louder than was needed. His slighting remarks about the French king were overheard by two burly men at arms seated further along the bench at our rough table. "Watch your mouth, monk," one of them said. "You should be respectful of the country that hosts you." The other, plainly drunk, snarled that he would teach this mouthy priest his manners, and stumbled to his feet. I too struggled upright, my feet tangling in the bench, but I was too late. The second soldier had drawn his blade and was threatening Adam's throat with it. I had neither time nor space to draw Bloodblade, so I backhanded the first man at arms across the face, sending him sprawling, even as I kicked the bench clear of my feet.

Above the clatter I heard a sharp wheeze and a spray of

blood spattered on my cheek. The drunk soldier had lunged the point of his sword into Adam's neck. He staggered back, but, a onetime soldier, he was dangerous even when mortally wounded. He slid the concealed punching knife from its sheath on his left forearm and as his attacker moved in stabbed upwards and hard under the ribs. It stopped the man in his tracks; I seized the fellow's shoulder and threw him backwards away from Adam and turned to my old companion. Matters were plain, his throat gaped and blood was spurting like a pump. The wound was certainly fatal.

Adam stumbled. I grasped at his arm and steered him towards a bench, where he sat heavily, slumping. Something hit me solidly in the nape of my neck and I turned to find the first man at arms drawing back his sword to strike me again with the heavy brass pommel. I kicked at his kneecap, he fell, twisting towards me just as his drunken comrade came back at me, surprisingly still upright despite the knife in his rib cage.

The fighting madness was on me, that familiar sparkling-bright time of heightened colour and clarity when you see and comprehend everything. It is a time when all goes so slowly you can foretell your opponent's next steps in a deadly, intuitive dance almost before he knows for himself what he will do. I pulled the falling man to me, a shield against his companion's sword. He struggled and I let my anger and strength flow. I was behind the man, and I seized a hank of his greasy black hair and jerked his head backwards, intending to disable him with a fisted blow across the throat. But he stumbled, off-balance and I jolted him down so that his head bounced against the side of the upturned bench.

He looked up at me, as mute as a sheep, his neck resting on the bench's side. He was dazed, his system shocked and unable for a moment to send the signals from his brain. Fast as a stoat, I stamped down with my booted foot, intending to pound his head and knock him unconscious, but even while my foot was in the air, he wriggled and half-fell sideways. My boot came down full force on the side of his neck where it rested on the impromptu executioner's block.

The separating vertebrae made an audible crack, the man's spine snapped and he was dead. His death rattle as the lungs emptied of air sounded loudly just as his slumping body rolled to the floor. I had no time to consider him again, the drunk was moving at me, his sword wet with Adam's blood. My own Bloodblade seemed to unsheath himself and leap into my fist.

The drunk, his movements fatally slowed by Adam's knife, which still protruded incongruously beneath the fellow's breastbone, scythed his sword at me. I brushed it aside, stamped forward and lunged. The point always beats the blade. It was the work of a moment more to kick Bloodblade free of the clinging muscles of the man's throat where my steel had transfixed it, and I could turn to Adam. One glance was enough. The pulsing, oxygen-bright arterial blood spurting from the big gash in his neck told me the cleric had only moments to live.

I clamped my hand over the wound in a forlorn attempt to seal it, but Adam, half-reclining against a table, communicated wordlessly with his eyes. He seemed to shake his head at my efforts. "You're going, old friend," I said. He blinked calmly, silently telling me that he understood and then, as easily as that, he slipped away to his long rest.

The next hour was confusion, noise and some drama. Two local men dead, and murdered by foreigners at that; a monk slain, a nobleman sword-fighting in a tavern…. Guillaume de FitzJohn, the Comte de Bosquet and one of our Crusader party, heard of the excitement and went to investigate. He was French, his holdings were in the region, and his power and influence were enough to sway the town's *bailli* not to arrest me. Witnesses who testified that the man at arms had drawn his sword first, and against an innocent monk at that, persuaded the local lord's seneschal to go along with the decision, and he allowed matters to drop. My own loudly-defiant vow that I would not allow anyone to arrest me, and the sight of my considerable size and weaponry all soaked in blood likely helped, too.

Fact was I knew I must, absolutely must, not be taken. I had secret treasures that had to be delivered and if it meant fighting my way out of the town I would do so.

We took Adam's body to the Ursuline nuns in their fine Roman building. They prepared him for interment and contacted some locals of his Benedictine brethren to conduct the rites. As I grasped his shoulder and said my farewell to his stiffening corpse, I registered for the first time that his monk's ruff of hair was silver. It seemed a marvel that I had not noticed it before. "You were becoming an old man, Adam," I murmured, "but you fought right at the end. God be with you, I'll see you in another time and place."

For myself, I knew I should soon be finding myself in another place. I dared not dally in Vezelay lest I face arrest by de Montfort's many allies, for word must have leaked out about the intent of our mission and we were not numerous enough to resist even the town constable and his forces should he be ordered to take us.

So it was that our small group clattered out of Vezelay for Toulouse at wolf light the next morning, our breakfasts of black bread and vast pork sausages stuffed in saddlebags to be consumed as we rode. I was bitterly saddened at the loss of my longtime friend, and trailed by a sense of shame at having to run from possible imprisonment. But I had the sword and the Shroud to consider and delivering them to Ramon and his forces was of paramount importance. I also had a most vital portable altar lashed to a packhorse and it contained a treasure for which de Montfort would have raised the hue and cry across all of France, had he but known...

Chapter XVIII: Toulouse
Frederick

Alaric said he was concerned about me. "You are more subdued than I have ever seen you," he said as we crossed Burgundy and headed for Ramon's capital and stronghold of Toulouse. I simply growled at him and told him to take his womanly concerns elsewhere, but secretly I acknowledged the truth of what he said. I have seen hundreds of men die, have lost a score or more of my closest companions and evaded death myself a handful of times. Dying does not scare me, and I suppose I'm shallow enough not to show much emotion over most things. I was hurt, or my pride was dented when Alaric's mother, Blanche, had told me she did not wish to renew our relationship, but then again, she was a nun and had been one for decades. I absorbed the news, shrugged it off and for old times' sake – and because I had great wealth now – gave her a large gift of stolen jewels and gold. In a day or so, I realized that actually I was relieved to be rid of her. I now had no responsibilities. Alaric and his sons would inherit my demesnes, I could get on with the interesting business of war.

Then Adam was killed, and the old monk's death hit me hard. He had been with me since boyhood and was about the last link to the good days of Lionheart, crusading joy and great glory.

"Are you sure we could not stay for Adam's funeral?" Alaric asked. He seemed hopeful that perhaps the situation was not as bad as any fool could see it was.

"Don't be an idiot, boy!" I snapped at him. "De Montfort has plenty of spies. He probably knows that we are not on our way to put down the Cathars, but instead we're travelling to kill him. He may not know that we are taking Tristan's sword and the Holy Shroud to rally a Cathar army, but he could find out. And if he did, my lord of Leicester, Earl Simon would kill every one of us without the least compunction, to get his hands on those objects.

"Our safety until now has been that he did not know we were travelling. Now, he certainly does. A monk's murder in a town full of pilgrims gets people talking, and unfortunately I've been identified, so that news too will go to him. We need to keep on the move."

So we went, and briskly, with me muttering an apology to the gallant old monk who was once a soldier and who had died a soldier's death. We moved swiftly and as unobtrusively as we could, taking directions from a leech-gatherer who paused in his work wading bare-legged in a muddy ditch. He climbed out, unconcernedly peeled off several of his slimy catches and for the reward of a small coin led us a mile across fields to point the way. At dusk we used the quiet local ferry he had revealed to us, and crossed the Loire. We did not wish to use any major bridge where our presence might have been reported, and so, we moved unhindered through the empty volcanic country south of Clermont.

We avoided the good basalt road built by the Romans as too likely to be monitored by de Montfort's men, and therefore dangerous; travelled cross-country through sere plains under a chain of dead volcanoes and at last slipped, anonymously cloaked and unnoticed into the pilgrim centre of Le Puy en Velay, entering through the city gates at dusk, just before they were closed and barred for the night.

Our French Templar, Guillaume FitzJohn, was familiar with the town and eager to tell us of it. "Le roi Louis Sept brought the statue of the black Virgin back here from the Second Crusade," he boasted. "She is in the cathedral above us." He rolled his eyes upwards where we could just see in the loom of the dark the magnificent cathedral was situated on a towering outcrop. The coloured glass windows, lit from inside by the candles of the faithful, seemed to glow not in welcome, but as ominously as the firelit eyes of a wolf. I shook off a shudder and halted us at the next auberge, where we found beds for the night in a smelly, noisy dormitory. The next-door tavern was even noisier and more odiferous but it was warm and had food for us. The Occitan language was being shouted to each other by locals eager to override the foreign tongues of the pilgrims.

We were truly in the Languedoc, region of the 'Language of the Oc', where the locals use the same accent as my departed friend Lionheart and say a rural 'Oc,' not 'Oui.' In a wave of unexpected nostalgia I remembered Richard's homely accent and the adventures we had enjoyed, and I smiled grimly as I recalled one that nearly killed us both. Lionheart, Europe's leading warrior, had been disarmed when his sword snapped and was forced to drive off a rabble of Calabrian villagers by throwing rocks at them while I stood stunned and bleeding, unable to fight. So much for Richard's ornamental sword that snapped off uselessly. I patted Bloodblade's hilt. He was reliable enough, and we were getting closer to our Cathar allies, so he would be in use soon. The innkeeper brought cold mutton, oatcakes hot from the griddle and a flagon of thin red wine, and we ate, contented that we were well along on our journey.

The next dawn, we were on the old Via Podiensis, moving south and west but I felt we were conspicuous riding our horses among the trudging pilgrims, so eventually turned our small group aside from their trail and onto the good iron road that led to Rodez, or so the tall, cylindrical mileposts left by the Romans informed us. From there we learned, the route went to Albi: the ancient stonemasons had chiselled 'Segondum,' and 'City of the Albigensians' into their markers.

"We'll sleep in Albi tomorrow night," I promised our troop, then spent minutes in sign language explaining the plan to the leader of the Hunnish archers. I was not sorry to get them away from curious eyes, for their unfamiliar appearance provided the kind of memorable and identifying detail an observer might pass to de Montfort's spies.

That night in yet another smelly tavern, I was speaking with a local trader who was impressed that an Englishman spoke Occitan and over several wooden pots of cider provided me with news of the region. He knew Albi, he'd been to market there to deliver *pastel*, bundles of insignificant little yellow flowers that form the basis for blue dye. He grew the plant and delivered me a sermon on crushing the leaves, moulding them into pressed balls and laying them down like wine to provide a more intense colour as they age. I was stifling yawns when he casually mentioned Toulouse, and how he had heard that Ramon, seigneur of the entire region, had been humiliated by the Catholic bishops. I paid instant attention.

When I could decipher what the increasingly drunken dye trader had to say, it appeared that Count Ramon had been held responsible for the death of a papal legate. Denied a trial, he had been forced to swear fealty to Rome after an especially humiliating ceremony.

Proud Ramon had been led naked through the streets of the city he ruled to the door of the church of St Gilles. There, in the presence of half a hundred churchmen he was forced to swear obedience to Rome. He was led by a rope around his neck to be scourged publicly by several bishops and only then was absolved of his 'sin.' But he had to pay more.

De Montfort had somehow influenced Pope Innocent to hand over Ramon's lands to him and to exile the count, who fled across the mountains to his overlord, the King of Aragon. There, he had gathered an army and soon returned to seize his old capital of Toulouse. The city fell to him without resistance, for de Montfort had abandoned it when his followers went home after their term of service ended for the year.

"They say an English king came a month or so ago, with an army to capture Toulouse for the count, but he wasn't needed and he took ship from Bordeaux to fight the Saracens," the old soak of a trader told me. My vitals went cold. The 'English king' was almost certainly my own overlord, Ranulf. If he had decided he was not needed and had carried on to Egypt, I had no troops waiting for me. All I could hope was that it was untrue.

Within two days, however, messengers who had been desperately tracking our concealed movements across France finally found us and confirmed the news. Earl Ranulf had opted to continue to Egypt, partly it seemed because Ramon appeared well-set inside his walls, and partly, to judge from the tone of one of Ranulf's messages to me, because the good

Earl had heard false tales of the Cathars approval of unnatural sexual practices. Ranulf wrote primly that he felt as a good Christian it would taint the purity of his crusade should he fight for Ramon.

"Christ's teeth and bones!" I was furious. Ranulf's piety had just cut the legs from under my military mission. He had taken my troops with him to Egypt on the strength of a rumour and a false one at that. We were left with no reinforcements to offer Ramon. "It's an especially vicious slander," I complained to Alaric. "The Cathar parfaits actually abstain from sex, they are the most decent, clean-living of all the Christians. Now, how are we going to fight de Montfort?"

Chapter XIX: Albi
Alaric

Twin watchtowers high above the River Tarn told our little party that we were approaching Albi. "They're to protect the wine barges that move down this river to the Garonne, and on to Bordeaux. We're not that far from the Atlantic," Frederick told me. "If anyone wants to go home instead of going on to Toulouse, that's your swiftest way back." Nobody responded, as I expected and we continued in silence.

We were riding to Tolouse after a year when the city had been besieged and surrendered, then rebelled and been besieged again. De Montfort had taken his campaign elsewhere and suffered his first major defeat. That was at Beaucaire, a loss that had been quickly followed at the end of 1216 by another defeat at Lourdes. The fighting had continued all winter, with Toulouse changing hands as the Catholic Crusaders forced the Cathars out under treaties of surrender, but as we approached on that crisp autumn day of 1217, messengers came to tell us that the citadel had changed hands yet again.

Count Ramon was back in possession of the city after a surprise crossing of the Garonne by an ancient dam and ford called Le Bazacle. The stroke had overwhelmed the token garrison and trapped de Montfort's family in the Chateau Narbonnais, the castle on the west side of the citadel, and considerably set back Simon's ambitions.

We rode in through the battered but intact city gates to find the count in fine spirits. He had tears in his eyes as he greeted us. "Frederick, old friend," and "Alaric, what a fine son you are! Your father must be proud!"

I felt my face go hot and heard Frederick mutter something noncommittal, then: "He's a full Templar now, Ramon."

"Yes, I see his surplice. He makes a magnificent soldier." And so the meeting went, with no recriminations from that fine man Count Ramon about the missing reinforcements, just practical conferences about defending the city now he had it in his possession again.

His first action was to remove de Montfort's family from the ducal quarters in the castle and to put them under guard in the Garden Tower, a pleasant place where lavender and grapes grew in the summer. Ramon resumed his occupation of his old quarters, and invited the crusader Templars from England to feast with him that night.

We changed our travel-fouled clothes and bathed, then reported to the great hall of the chateau. Frederick asked for a private audience with the count, and asked me to accompany them, and puzzled, he motioned us to follow. We stepped into the cool dark of the chapel, and Frederick moved back to the door where a man at arms waited with a bundled package. I noted that he had an armed escort with him.

Frederick handed the bundle to me, indicating with a nod to hand it to Ramon. "My son, you have dedicated your life to God," he said. "It is appropriate that you give this to the count in this holy place." As I received the bundle, I knew what it was, and passed it with due reverence to the count. He, puzzled, unwrapped the Sword of Tristan. I thought he would faint. He handled it with awe, then placed it on the small altar of the chapel while Frederick explained its significance as a token of the support of the English barons and magnates.

Ramon bowed and murmured, his eyes glistening with tears, that he would be honoured to act as regent to the boy Henry. Frederick and he embraced, I too received the kiss of peace from the count, and while we embraced, Frederick went again to the chapel door. "Bring it in," he said brusquely and two armed men carried in a flat cedar wood box half the length of a man and an armspan wide. "Put it over there," said Frederick, gesturing. "Now leave us. Send in the Englishmen."

When the handful of Templars, the fighting friars – Gardiner, Grimshaw, Fitzjohn and myself, plus Frederick, St Denys, Barnstaple and FitzMorris, our old comrades who had made the rendezvous at Toulouse, were all mustered, Frederick asked everyone to kneel and join him in a prayer.

"We have in this box the most sacred icon of Christianity. It is with the inspiration of this winding sheet that we shall raise another army, because we have here traces of Christ's own body and blood to protect and guide us. We cannot fail in our enterprises, because we will be wrapped in Christ's love."

He began to open the case and I glanced at Ramon, who was utterly pale. As Frederick, aided by his old friend Berlage St Denys, carefully lifted out the Shroud of Christ, Count Ramon clutched the altar rail to steady himself. "Is this, the true Shroud, the one rescued by Joseph of Arimathea?"

My father nodded solemnly. "The very one," he said quietly.

"But how did you come by it?" the count demanded.

Frederick turned to me: "You tell him, my son," he said.

"Lord," I began, stammering, then rallied. "The knights of the Fourth Crusade entered Constantinople a dozen years ago and invaded the Boucoleon Palace where the Shroud was displayed. It had been appropriated somehow by the Byzantines, a century before, perhaps after the fall of Jerusalem.

"Who is responsible we do not know. There was slaughter and the Shroud vanished from Constantinople. Pope Innocent was greatly angered that Christians should so badly treat fellow Christians, even heretic ones, and I believe whoever took the relic was reluctant to own up to possessing it, for fear of excommunication for violence or looting. I know little else," I said lamely, stopping suddenly. The silence dragged for an age.

Finally, Frederick coughed quietly. "Seigneur Ramon," he said, "I can only tell you that it came to me secretly and for no reward just when we needed help to ensure the throne of England. If this holiest of holy relics can inspire an army and re-establish your authority, *Deus Vult*, you will be the agent to protect the boy who is our king."

Ramon had stepped forward and was gazing in evident awe at the long length of linen now spread fully out, revealing its mysterious markings. I noted that he did not touch it. A swift glance around told me that every single one of the armoured warriors in the chapel was equally entranced. All, that is, except Frederick, who, with a half-smile on his lips, was surreptitiously scanning the group. He seemed to be relishing the moment.

"This is, is so magnificent," Ramon almost stammered. "We should take it to the new pope, Honorius, and ask his blessing and the gift of peace. Perhaps the presentation of such a priceless memorial of Our Lord, will persuade him to tell de Montfort to call off the violence and maybe," he sounded wistful, "return some of my confiscated lands. They say he is a gentle, kind pope," he added hopefully.

"An excellent idea," Frederick boomed. "I'll take it there myself." Then he added: "Won't we, Alaric?" I nodded, dumbly, secretly horrified. We'd go to Rome and meet the Pope? I nodded again. I was a Templar knight, I was taking one of Christendom's most precious relics to Christ's vicar on Earth. Why did I have such doubts? But I recalled Frederick's small smile as he viewed my fellow monks gazing at the Shroud, and a deep unease settled somewhere below my ribcage.

Chapter XX: Montfort Frederick

Within a week, de Montfort was back at the gates of Toulouse, but we were ready. Years before, he had razed many of the villages to the north, around Albi but we had rebuilt them. Now the region of the Tarn had a dozen or more fortified villages we called *bastides*. They are protected places built between land and sky, places like Cordes sur Ciel, Castelnau, Puycels and Penne that could resist a siege, partly because their approaches were too difficult for an attacker's lumbering siege train.

From these centres of resistance came fighting men with hatred in their hearts for the despoiler of the region. They remembered with cold fury that fellow Frenchman had burned the *parfaits* and *bonhommes* alive, had mutilated women and children and left a trail of destruction, rape and plunder that had befouled the fairest part of France, and they tramped to Toulouse to join the forces that would turn back the marauders.

Count Ramon had acted while de Montfort was distant, campaigning in the valley of the Drome. In late 1217 Ramon returned across the Pyrenees to his capital with an army drawn from his holdings in Aragon. The count had surprised the citadel's small garrison and retaken the city. Our small group arrived only days later, then, on our heels, came the first of de Montfort's advance guard. They reached the battered walls too late, our frantic rebuilding of the defences was enough to hold them off and both sides settled in for a winter of blood, fire and siege.

"The siege of a city is just like a dance," I told my son Alaric, although I suspect he knew as much about the subject as I did. "There are moves and counter-moves, a ritual that has to proceed in certain pre-ordained steps. The outcome is certain if the steps are followed, but if there are errors, or conditions which cannot be overcome, then a siege will fail. It is our tasks to create those errors for Earl Simon."

The next few weeks were relatively peaceful. De Montfort was busy with his approach earthworks that would let him move siege engines closer to the walls. He was building palisades, to ring and contain the city. Within the walls, we were busy supervising the citizenry who were rebuilding and reinforcing the defences, and were drilling the soldier volunteers, in addition to digging wells and bringing in as many cattle and supplies as we could before the enemy encircled us.

Ramon ordered the Shroud sent in solemn procession through Toulouse each day, and word of the fervour it inspired spread though the countryside and attracted more men to our cause. Those outsiders reported that Bishop Fulk, an ally of de Montfort, was preaching the cross elsewhere in France and that men were flocking to his standard for the promise of land and plunder. Nonetheless, the evening procession of the Shroud gathered and encouraged the faithful, and the streets thronged with crowds eager to be blessed under its shadow.

The clergy were delighted at the new fervour, the recruiting serjeants were kept busy and the new troops drilled in a haze of devotion and hope that they were under the protection of heaven. It was a far cry from the previous visit to Toulouse by de Montfort, and Alaric pointed it out.

"We have been fortunate to have the greed of de Montfort opposing us," Alaric said dryly.

"What do you mean?" I asked sharply.

"Well, the last time he was here, he used fire and steel in an attempt to subdue the citizens and they fought him. Bishop Fulk interceded and suggested that the townspeople could earn his favour and stop the destruction if they paid 30,000 marks.

"De Montfort was exhausted, his money had gone on his earlier campaigns, and the prospect of a treasure of silver appealed to him. He used harsh measures, his typical cruelty, to get the levy. He flogged and punished those who held out and painted the doors of the citizens to show who had not paid so further punishments could be exacted against them. The Toulousians groaned under the lash and wished for the return of Count Ramon, so when he did arrive, he at once had their support and cooperation."

Spies brought us news of the growing strength of de Montfort's force, and I resolved to deliver some of the unexpected setbacks to him that we would need if we were to survive the siege. I approached Count Ramon but he was adamant: the thing to do was for me to deliver the Sword of Tristan to the King of Aragon. "You are an English baron. Tell him how this represents the promise of your fellow English to support me, tell him it is my humble wish that he send more troops to Toulouse, and lead them here yourself. If he does not respond to that, point out that it is his holy duty to rescue the Shroud from the sinful northerners who might use it next as their battle standard, and invade his territory behind it. Go soon, before snow fills the passes, and bring back an army in the early spring, when you can again cross the mountains."

It seemed a sensible plan. De Montfort would not have mustered enough men before late spring to force the siege, so for now, Ramon was safe enough inside Toulouse. I'd take a few knights and a small troop of cavalry to Zaragoza, where the young king James – a boy of 10 or so – was protected by the Templars and the regent Sancho of Rousillon. He was the third recent child ruler: our own Henry of Winchester held the throne of England at age nine; Henry of Castille had been killed by a falling roof tile just a few months before, when he was only weeks past his 13th birthday, and now we had James on the throne of Aragon. I would have to deal with his hard-eyed regents, so I decided that Alaric would stay in Toulouse with Ramon. I was becoming uncomfortable that my son might have guessed there was something suspicious about my conveniently 'found' icons and I wanted no hint of that when I met the Spanish with Tristan's sword.

The other thing I had to do before leaving France was to make a proper assessment of de Montfort's forces, which were swelling weekly, so I could carry that to Zaragoza, and to help us estimate when he could be ready to attack Toulouse. I took meticulous note of de Montfort's siege preparations. He would have difficulty digging his approach trenches through the flinty soil and we had plans to burn them before he could deploy the great wicker baskets he would fill with dirt and rocks as moveable shields to protect the sappers from our archers.

He had not yet begun to make the platforms or to fill the ditches he would need levelled so he could wheel his huge siege engines close to the walls, nor had he even begun the ramps and protective wheeled roofs he would need. Better still, he would have to bring from a distance the heavy timbers he'd need for his siege towers, big catapults and assorted ballistae. "He'll also have to travel to find the rocks he needs as missiles," said Alaric who seemed to be reading my thoughts.

"Two months, maybe three," I said.

"Agreed," said Alaric, and I recalled with a small shock that this son of mine was a seasoned soldier who had warred across Europe.

"Time enough for me to go and fetch an army," I said.

"Good idea," said Alaric, squeezing my arm. "Fetch one for me, too."

"Pray for us," I said lightly. "Use my little altar so the prayers find me." I did not want to travel to Spain with the coronation jewels that were hidden in the altar. That treasure would be safest with Alaric inside the city walls.

Cloaked and with our steeds' hoofs muffled, we slipped out of a postern gate after dark: the Frenchman FitzJohn de Bosquet; the indomitable old knight Jacquin de Grimshaw and the southerner Sir John Gardiner, all three of them Templars. My unstated purpose was to use Templars to reinforce the bond we wanted to establish with King James' own warrior friars.

We had a small troop of cavalry with us, and we elected to travel light and discreetly folded away our Templar surplices. I had appropriated one despite the sidelong looks of my companions who did not appreciate such a ruse de guerre, or my unqualified use of their sacred insignia, but they kept silent, and we rode in light mail without display of insignia or gonfalon to identify us. In those wild mountains, few would dispute with an armed and mailed party such as ours. Once in

Aragon, we would reconsider matters.

The cloak of darkness was kind, and we were soon out of the environs of the city unchallenged and making good time for the Pyrenees, which we reached unhindered after three days' hard riding. There we took on two guides who led us over sheep tracks and up steep mountain trails before we began a plunge down to the territory of the Vicomtes de Bearn.

"We have to go this way, lord," one of the guides explained. "The Gave is a torrent, a very difficult river to cross and the ford at Pau is the only one for a long day's ride." As we came off the mountain we saw in the distance the gleam of the palisade which gave the place its name. The wooden wall stood below the newly-built chateau on its small eminence that overlooks both the crossing and the valleys of the Bearn. The new chateau completely controls and dominates the chokepoint for the whole region.

It must be a place accustomed to travelers, I thought, and I was already planning where we'd stay for the night and what we would eat, when the first arrows whistled out of the gathering dusk.

FitzJohn died swiftly, choking and coughing as he drowned in his own blood. A crossbow bolt had transfixed his throat and his gore was spouting like pumped water, sheeting him crimson. Grimshaw was also on the ground, an arrow shaft sticking incongruously from his left eye, his great sword Bonecrusher in hand, circling blindly to keep any attacker at bay. Next to him, Gardiner was tugging at an arrow that protruded from his thigh. My destrier was rearing and bucking, from the two shafts that had penetrated his neck, and that probably saved my life. His erratic movements wrecked our ambushers' aim, and the broad-bladed arrow that struck me only in the ribs, where my mail shirt took most of the force. The arrow broke through, but did not penetrate as deeply as it might have. I groped to find the shaft, took a deep breath and snapped it off, grunting at the pain but I needed unimpeded motion of my sword arm.

My horse was still passaging about, and I heeled him hard to force him around, but he refused and by the time I had successfully jerked his head about, five of our men at arms were supine on the rocky ground, felled by arrows or slingers' deadly, egg-sized leaden missiles. Two of the remaining three were kneeling, one coughing blood, the other holding his face in his hands. Bitterly, I recognised that the ambush had been a near-total success. In moments, of the dozen of us, only two of my knights and one cavalryman had survived. Even as I was sweeping my glance around to assess matters, two brigands seized my horse's head and a third, materializing from behind a boulder, seized my foot and heaved me out of the saddle and painfully onto the ground.

The next I knew was the stink of garlic breath and a misericorde point at my eye. "Stay still, sweetheart," growled some ruffian in Occitan, "or I prick your eyeball." I stayed still.

The ambush had been laid by a brigand band of two dozen mixed archers and men at arms, led by a dark-visaged, wolfish ruffian who knew his business. They quickly bound us, ran a sword into FitzJohn to ensure he was dead and slit the throats of the unfortunate, dying cavalrymen of our troop. I saw one laugh as he wrenched the arrow from Grimshaw's eye socket, causing the Templar to pass out with pain, then two more of the archers were lashing my wrists in front of me before they went through my possessions for loot.

They took Bloodblade, which they handed over to the bandit chief and quickly found the false Sword of Tristan and took that to him, too. In minutes, they had a pile of our arms and possessions on the sheep-nibbled turf and were crowing over the several purses of silver they'd found.

My side was pounding from the arrowhead that was between my ribs and I was dizzy and weak, fighting to stay alert. The wolfish brigand came to me carrying Tristan's sword. "Where do you take this?" he asked in passable Occitan.

"It is nothing, just a trophy from Constantinople," I said, shaking my head.

"It is a special sword," he insisted. I cursed myself for mentioning Constantinople. I should have said almost anywhere else. "I think this is the religious sword," the brigand said thoughtfully. "We heard there was a sword, the sword of Vivar, being taken to the new Queen of Spain since the young king died."

"Oh, that is bad news," I said innocently, "did Henry of Castille die?"

The brigand eyed me sardonically. "Yes, the poor boy. He hit his head. In the spring. You must have heard."

I shook my head. "I have been travelling." It was a feeble lie and we both knew it.

"Perhaps, then," said the ruffian, elaborately polite, "I could save you more travel. I could deliver the sword for you." Several of the listening soldiers laughed at the exchange.

"That would be an excellent suggestion," I mumbled through my clenched teeth.

"Right," he straightened up. "Tie him to the tail of my horse," he nodded at me and strode away to supervise the other captives. Within a quarter hour, we were being dragged along, ever downwards, into the valley of the Bearn, and to my surprise to the chateau of the count who ruled the region. We arrived after dark, splashing through a ford, then wending through a maze-like defensive stockade inside which was a cobbled forecourt to the new castle. The horses clattered across it to halt at iron-bound gates that were lit by bales of burning hay. It was not too soon. I was painfully footsore, my wrists were bleeding and my shoulders ached from being dragged at a horse's tail, my side was torn and painful from the arrow-strike and I was weak from blood loss. "But you are alive," I told myself.

Chapter XXI: Pau
Frederick

The cell was chill, dank, and stank of stale urine and vomit,
but exhaustion and blood loss helped me to sleep soundly
on a paillasse stuffed with rotting straw, and for all my aches
and wounds I felt almost refreshed when the door was
banged open by two men at arms. They hauled me to my feet,
manacled me and pushed me outside where, perhaps mindful
of my size, two more guards waited, spears lowered. They led
me up flights of stone steps to a hall where a stocky man in
an embroidered tunic sat in a throne on a small dais. "Kneel
to the visconte Raumes," one of my jailers growled, pushing
me in the back. I stumbled to my knees. The nobleman looked
down at me. "You carry a Templar surcoat but do not wear
it," he said. "Why is this? Why do you travel like a spy? Who is
your master?"

The man irritated me and I glared up at him. "You have
murdered my men, killed a Crusader, wounded two more of
us, all this against the law of the Church and the declared
Peace of God and you question me about my condition?" I
spat at the fellow's feet. My action drew a swift reaction and
I was stunned and knocked sideways by a blow to the temple

from the butt end of one of the guards' spears. Through the roaring in my ears I heard him saying something about my lack of respect for my betters but I was too dazed to care.

The visconte, for it was indeed the petty ruler of Bearn, came down from his little throne and kicked me thoughtfully in my wounded ribs then hissed as I leaked blood on his precious antependia, an altar hanging he was using as a carpet in front of the podium. The next half hour went on much as the initial confrontation did, with the guards beating me, the little tyrant demanding information and me too weary to care or respond. Finally, the visconte gave up. "Bring the other chevalier," he said, and de Grimshaw was dragged in. He looked as I felt.

He had been arrow-blinded in one eye then hacked about by blades as he fought our ambushers, and he had sustained some nasty wounds. His skin was the colour of a Greyfriar's robe and without the assistance of the men at arms who supported him it seemed he would collapse to the floor. Raumes wasted no time. "What is this sword?" he demanded, waving the Tristan weapon in de Grimshaw's face.

"Put it down," the Templar said. "It's for a man, not some worm pervert like you." The blow the visconte aimed would have severed Grimshaw's neck had it been properly delivered. As it was, the flat of the blade smacked into the Templar's skull and dropped him unconscious.

The visconte turned to me again. "Where were you taking this?"

"I never knew," shrugged. That earned me a swift bout of unconsciousness and when I came around I'd been dragged to the fighting platform inside the crenellations of the ramparts.

De Grimshaw was slumped at spearpoint against a wall, our one surviving trooper was bound, hooded and held by two spearmen alongside him. The wind was bitingly cold and to my irritation I shivered. "Afraid, Templar?" the visconte, warmly fur-wrapped as I sourly noticed, was watching me.

"Go and swive your pig," I said.

"You'll talk," he said confidently. "Move him," this to the spearmen who had our one trooper by the arms. They pushed him to the parapet wall and one dropped a halter around his neck and slid the noose snug. Horrified, I let my eyes follow the long rope back. It was tied off to a grille. The trooper, whose breath movements I could see sucking at the linen hood over his head, was swaying precariously over the parapet, held upright by one of the spearmen. "Again," said the visconte, "who is to receive that sword, and what does it mean? I know it is from Constantinople, it must be something important, maybe even sacred."

My voice croaked. "You are breaking the Peace of God, your soul is in mortal danger." It was all I could think to say, and it sounded desperate.

"Push him," Raumes ordered and the trooper made a yelping noise as he pitched head-first over the parapet. The sound ended a second after it began, cut off in a horrible choking gurgle as the rope went rigid and the noose bit. The rope sawed at the parapet edge, then steadied. "Pull him up." It took three spearmen to haul the corpse up, its breeches fouled, the head lolling at an odd angle, a trickle of blood from the bitten-through tongue. It was no longer a man, just a shell, a cadaver. I'd seen a lot of them.

The visconte was watching me, and seemed unsatisfied, then gestured at de Grimshaw. "His feet," he said simply. In moments, the guards had lashed my comrade's bare feet to a heavy bench, higher than his head, and one villain stood waiting with a rawhide whip. "Beat him," said the visconte, and a guard lashed de Grimshaw's feet brutally. In moments, his feet were ridged and raw, another minute and the skin burst. Blood ran onto his ankles and dripped steaming onto the flagstones, but de Grimshaw neither screamed nor spoke although his whole body was shuddering.

Raumes looked closely at him. "What is this sword?" he demanded. The crusader raised his bound wrists to his face and deliberately pushed his thumb into his mouth in an obscene gesture. The defiance inflamed Raumes. He waved forward the largest of the guards. "Take that thumb. He will never do that ever again." The spearman almost casually took de Grimshaw's hand in his own two great paws, seized the fingers in one hand and the thumb in the other. He made a swift, hard downward wrench and snapped the thumb backwards against the joint closest to the palm. The sharp crack as the bone broke was echoed by an agonised groan from de Grimshaw, who slumped unconscious from the pain.

I looked on horrified. The thumb dangled loose, held only by muscle and flesh. Raumes gestured. "Take it right off." A second soldier stepped forward, pulled out his dagger and began sawing at the digit, which he hacked off raggedly. He stood, holding the bloody lump of flesh, indecisive. Raumes was watching, fascinated. De Grimshaw stirred, opened his good eye.

"Take him to the wall," Raumes said, pointing.

I drew myself up and said as urgently as I could: "Heed me, visconte. Your immortal soul is in great danger. This contravenes the pope's own peace. Stop now before you condemn yourself to eternity in the flames." The stocky little bastard grinned at me.

"I'll not tell the pope," he said. "Nor will you. Now, finally, tell me about the sword. It is someone's, it is not just a weapon, is it?"

De Grimshaw, blinded, dripping blood, and swaying, somehow rallied himself. "Tell the devil's turd nothing," he said thickly. "Forget his shriveled soul. His stinking body is in mortal danger from me once I get this rope off." The visconte waved a hand and three men at arms pushed the Templar to the parapet. He could barely stand on his bloodied, raw feet. All it would take was one short shove.

"I have to do it, Jacquin," I said to my old comrade. "I'm telling him."

And I did. I told of the Sword of Tristan, I even admitted it was a fake, that it had not come from Constantinople, but the visconte did not believe that. I told of why I had it made, of the regent, of the boy king of England, of the army I hoped it would raise to save Ramon and Toulouse. I offered a fortune in gold, made a promise of land. Finally, I fell silent. The visconte chewed at his lip and nodded, then casually turned to his soldiers. "Over with him," he said. That gallant English Templar, de Grimshaw turned his head and grinned at me even as he was thrust across the parapet to his death. He made no sound, he went as he lived, in courage and faith.

My own fury at this betrayal gave me new strength and I fought my guards, bound as I was. I choked one guard with my manacles, and lunged at Raumes but did not reach him. Two guards hung onto my bindings but I managed to spit copiously into the visconte's face. A guard battered my eye, I head-butted him, smashed the cheekbone of a second with an elbow and bit several others as they swarmed me while the visconte scuttled to safety. I came back to consciousness in my cell with broken ribs, fingers and nose, two closed eyes, a lumpy skull and a variety of cuts and small slash wounds. I thought I'd lost an eye but it turned out to be merely a cut eyelid that had drooped.

After an hour or two, four guards came in and forced my wrists together so that my left arm was above and over my left shoulder and skewed into the small of my back. My right arm was twisted up below its shoulder so both wrists met to be manacled. Then the fatherless bastards hoisted me onto a wall hook in the corner of the cell and tensioned the fetters so that only my toes reached the floor.

My wounded ribs seemed about to burst and I was desperately aware that I still had an arrowhead in my side. The pain in my back, ribs and shoulders was excruciating and my whole body felt as if it would snap at any moment. For the first age, I was able to push up with my toes to relieve some of the pressure, but as my feet cramped and my toes lost strength, more weight came onto my ribs and I was suffocating like a crucified man. I had to suck air down into my lungs through a fog of burning pain. There came the scrape and creak as the cell door opened and Raumes came in. I could barely see him through my swollen eyes.

He approached me cautiously and spat full into my face. "I will teach you manners, you pig," he said. "Hang there for a while and consider how to make your apologies. Give him a drink. Keep him alive."

One of the guards chuckled and left the cell, returning with a wooden pail full of water. "Have a drink on us, brave chevalier," he said and threw the water over me. It was no hardship. My lips were split and parched and the water was surprisingly sweet and cool and felt good. I soaked in every drop I could, then slumped my head in pretended semi-consciousness.

The guards left, I listened until all was quiet, then began exploring my situation. I pushed my bare foot backwards and found a toehold in the wall, a level of protruding stone no thicker than the back of a blade. I stretched out my other foot, inching it carefully and battling to ignore the flares of pain in my shoulders. I moved it along the right angle of the corner. There was another ripple of rock, just enough for my foot to gain a miniscule purchase. Carefully I eased my toes onto the two small protuberances. By pushing back hard on the right, I could press myself against the wall below the hook and with that as balance could push myself up on the agonised other foot. All this painful effort earned little, but it did allow me to edge myself a handspan higher off the cell floor. My toes hurt like fire, but my shoulder pains were considerably eased as the manacles slackened.

With the new slack, I could just barely grope my fingers over the bracelet of the manacle. It had a simple turnkey, nothing elaborate, and by locking my knuckles I could wrap them around it for a grip. Then my foot slipped and I fell, just a handful of inches, but an agonizing drop onto my tortured shoulder. I hung gasping until the burn was manageable, then struggled back onto my two small ledges. An age later, I fell again and scraped myself back up again. Thank Thor for the warrior's muscles of my shoulders and back, muscles that tolerated the agony without tearing.

Finally, several lifetimes later, gasping with pain and soaked in sweat despite the chill of the cell, I succeeded in revolving the pivot, and the fetter ran free. One manacle fell open, the pressure instantly eased and I stumbled forward into the cell. For two full, agonizing minutes I waited, fearful that the chain's rattle had alerted a guard. If one came in now, I was unable to fight. My agonisingly stiff upper body made me helpless. But nobody came.

I worked my frozen shoulders and back, forcing hot blood through the strained, abused muscles until I could move. I stripped off my tunic and formed it with the paillasse and the water pail into as convincing a facsimile of a hanging human form as I could and suspended it from the corner hook. Fortunately, dusk was approaching and the cell had no window. A careless glance would seem to confirm that I was still suspended in the dark corner. Then, after considering the angles of vision from the Judas hole in the door, I sat on the floor where I thought I would be invisible if the guards peeped in before entering.

My captors had long since found the punching knife I kept hidden at the nape of my neck, and had taken it, but they left the blood-fouled strap and sheath that had held it. I took off both. I had use for them. Then, massaging my limbs, I sat in the near-dark and listened for the guard. An hour or so later, he came, with a flickering rushlight that shone under the door.

Thor smiled on me. They sent only one jailer and I could tell it from the sound of his footfall. I was on my feet in the shadows waiting as he unbarred the door. It was the bigger of my two regular jailers and he had a bucket in one hand, the rushlight in the other. I just had time to glance to confirm that he was alone before I was pressing the knife's rigid sheath into his jugular. "Make noise and die," I whispered. "Lower the bucket slowly to the floor." He nodded his head and obeyed. As he was bending, I was slipping his knife from his belt. As he straightened, my left hand went around his head and covered his mouth, I jerked him backwards onto his own blade, sliding it upwards under the ribcage to puncture his heart. He bit my hand deeply as he struggled, but I did not release and he died with little more than what sounded like a conversational gurgle.

I ran my hands though his pockets, took his belt and knife sheath, swore as I found he was wearing around his neck my own silver mjollnir, the little Thor's hammer he had stolen, and took it back. I also took his helmet, leather jerkin and nailed boots, all of which fitted me reasonably well and put everything on in the privacy of the cell. Finally, I dragged the body across to the corner wall hook and, grunting with effort, hung him there. I draped my tunic over him, barred the cell door behind me and moved quietly down the hallway. At the end where another hall crossed, I could hear the rattle of dice and a cup and bursts of raucous laughter. The guardroom. I moved the opposite way, ducked up a stone stairway when I heard someone approaching and padded quietly, knife drawn, along another hall.

Cooking smells and chatter from one direction, the crackle and spit of a fire from the other. I went that way. A door was partly open, but my view inside the chamber was blocked by a draught-excluding heavy hanging across the inside of the doorway. I cautiously moved an edge of the hanging aside. The room was lit by the fire and several large candles. The room's only occupant was a man who was seated with his back to me, flicking a length of yarn and playing with a kitten. I slid into the room. The man moved as he toyed with the cat, I glimpsed his face and realized it was the visconte Raumes himself. I reached behind myself, groping for the door's latch, my fingers found the bolt and I slid it locked.

An especially loud hiss and crackle from the fire spat

an ember out, and as Raumes half-rose from his chair to extinguish it in the rushes that covered the floor, I was across the space and had my hands around his throat. He stared in shock into my face and I brought up my knee and drove it with all my force into his crotch. I still had his throat as he crumpled to his knees, eyes wide in agony.

"The sword," I hissed, "where is it?" Raumes' face was stark white with shock and pain. His mouth gaped open, his tongue swelling, making an arc. His hands came up weakly to clutch my wrists. "The sword!" I spat at him again. His eyes rolled sideways and he tried to turn his head. I followed his attempt. A sword stood against the end of the fireplace. I released Raumes and as he slid downwards knee'ed him viciously in the temple, driving him sideways, unconscious. He half rolled in the rushes, and the kitten pounced in play on his foot. A quick look around the room. Another door over there. I took the few paces to the fireplace to grasp the sword that leaned against it. Wrong sword. Not the sword of Tristan, but my own familiar Bloodblade. He felt good and strong and confidence-enhancing in my grip.

I looked down at the visconte. Still out cold. There was little time for decisions, I knew I had to act swiftly and with determination. I could take the unconscious man with me – easier said than done – as hostage, or I could flee. Could I find Tristan's sword without the visconte? Probably not. Faster than it takes to tell, I resolved to flee. But first, I reversed Bloodblade and aimed him, point down, two hands on his leather-wrapped hilt, and pushed him into the hollow under Raumes' throat. The jab of pain roused the man and his eyes opened. He stared up at me. "Undo your breeches," I said. He fumbled his clothes open. "Say goodbye world, and bid hello to Hell," I spat at him and leaned on my sword, driving it clear through the throat and out of the nape of his neck. He could not shout, his voice box was destroyed and although he thrashed like a landed pike I held him transfixed for the single minute it took for him to bleed out.

Then I pushed Bloodblade into my belt and drew the soldier's dagger. A swift hooking motion and one violent, strong pull and the sharp blade had severed the dying visconte's testicles. "You'll be speaking like an unbroken boy when you pass Jacquin on your way to the Devil," I said, and I spat in his face one more time.

There was a discreet knocking at the locked door behind me. "Raumie?" a woman's voice was saying.

"Go away, I'm busy," I growled

But the voice said with an alarmed note: "Is that you, *mon ange*?" I slipped out of the other door.

Leaving the chateau was easier than I could have hoped. I had the guard's jerkin and helmet and a drawn sword to cloak me in anonymity and for luck touched my Thor's hammer, returned now to its rightful place at my throat. Deliberately, I made much clatter with the nailed boots as I ran down the stone stairways, shouting for guards to the main hall, now! A rush of spearmen from the gatehouse went by, I smelled then found the stable, seized two horses and had them haltered in moments. I didn't bother with a saddle, swung aboard one horse and led the other and trotted without seeming haste under the portcullis and through the palisades unchallenged. We clattered into the street, plunged through the ford and headed for the frosty slopes of the valley side before any pursuit showed.

After a steady climb under a half-moon, I turned the horse's head south. Any pursuit, any hue and cry would likely aim east, back to France. So I went south along the spine of the mountains that mark the border. With luck, I could turn east for France before any patrol that knew of the visconte's murder could intercept me.

And so, I made my way back over the mountains to report my failure at Toulouse. I wondered what I could say about Sir John Gardiner. When last I saw him he was wounded and about to be overwhelmed by brigands. For the rest of our small party, all were dead, and the sword, vital symbol of those committed to an English rebellion, was lost. My soul felt as battered as my body.

Chapter XXII: Refuge
Frederick

Chancing across the friar was a fine stroke of luck, made better by the lonely surroundings. He was a Dominican, a travelling, teaching friar and his white tunic and scapular struck me at once as an excellent colour in that snowy landscape for a fugitive who wished to avoid pursuers or other confrontations. I'd made my plans long before we halted facing each other, he on his mule, me bareback and leading another steed.

I must have looked like a horse thief, but he was trustingly unsuspicious of me, although my bloodied and bruised appearance, too, should have alerted him. Faith is a fine thing. "Help me, father," I said. "I have been attacked by brigands." That at least was true. From shame at how I treated that good man, I'll pass over the next few minutes, but they ended with him trussed with his own black leather belt, wrapped in his mule's blanket and missing his purse, food and outer clothes.

In a half hour or so he should be able to wriggle free and walk unharmed a fair distance to habitation, in the meantime, I was a white friar with two horses, a mule, a full belly and a sword concealed under my habit. The scapular I was now wearing, the Dominican mournfully told me, is a blessed protective shield of purity bestowed by the Holy Virgin, and was not to be regarded as a workman's apron. I thanked him cheerfully and hoped it would protect me as it had protected him – he was still alive, after all. He nodded, bit his lip and was obviously struggling to contain his sinful resentment as I rode away.

To confuse any who might find him and track me, I rode east while he could see me, but circled south again once I was free of his view. I rode the shaggy horses gently, aware that fodder might not be easily obtained and trotted across two steep, winding cols before a steady descent into the deep valley of a river I later learned was the Aspe. I could see from the smoke ahead of me that the settlement was not large, but instinct made me turn away from the easier road south and to head more westerly. On a whim I opted to head for a symmetrical pyramid of a peak that towered above the other mountains.

The countryside was karst, there was little forage for my animals, and I was weakening from the arrowhead I still carried in my ribs. Another night or two in the freezing cold could finish me. As the light began to fade from the short winter afternoon, I took my chances and rode towards a small village, hoping to bribe them with the monk's purse or even my horses to give me secret shelter.

A woman was stacking fuel in a woodpile outside her small stone house as I rode wearily up and she gazed at me in alarm.

"Brigands," I said in Occitan. "I am hurt."

"Oh, father," she said, "let me help." Just in time, I remembered I was a monk and murmured a "Bless you, my child," as she helped me down from my nag. I still had enough instinct left to ask where we were. "This is Areta," she told me. "It's rightly named. It means 'stony place' and it is a hard place to live."

"This is in Bearn?" I asked cautiously.

"Diocese of Oloron, father," she said briskly. "We are Count Ramon's people." I must have exhaled loudly, for she looked sharply at me.

"May the saints be praised," I said. "Ramon of Toulouse is my patron."

"I once lived in Toulouse," she said proudly, unselfconsciously helping me remove my habit so she could examine my rib wounds. "You came to the right person for this. I served in the Benedictines' hostel there." Her story came out as she bathed and dressed my wounds. An orphan left for the church to care for, she had some minimal training as an apothecary in the hostel operated for the city's poor and had been sent four years before as part of a mission to tend the flock in the Pyrenees. The preacher friar and his acolyte had died in a snowstorm, the girl was left alone and had stayed in this small village. Her name was Carole d'Outram, she was a comely young woman with dark hair, bold eyebrows and a confident way. She shook her head when I asked if she had a husband. "None here to like," she said.

"I wanted to go to Barcelona or Toledo but foreign apothecaries must prove they have plied their trade for at least a decade before they can be licensed there, it's because of the dangers of spices and poisons. You must prove your skills lest you do hurt to someone. It's all about knowledge of simples and compounds." She spoke absently as she worked. "I know about the cures of Hildegard of Bingen and of Rabbi Moses Maimonides. What they would do with this arrowhead would be to soak it in honey, tie a linen strip to it and ease it through to the other side. It hurts, but otherwise you'll die. I do not want to do that here because there is bone in the way and we could do more harm.

"What I can do is to enlarge the wound it has made, grip the shaft of the arrowhead with thin tongs and bring it out the way it went in. I can give you something to help the pain, and afterwards I'll dress the wound in a poultice of barley, mint, honey and turpentine to prevent the flesh from rotting."

I gritted my teeth and nodded. "Do it," I said. I had seen too many men die of suppurating wounds. Leaving the arrowhead in place was a death sentence.

Carole made up an infusion of yarrow to soothe the brain; poppy and hemlock to dull the inevitable hurt, and chamomile to reduce any fever. Then she crushed some cone-shaped hop flowers into the brew, to ease me into sleep. I swallowed the draught – not too unpleasant – and she continued to work on my battered eyes and facial cuts while it took effect. She was splinting my broken fingers when I somehow drifted off into a sleep that was disturbed by strange dreams of black-clad men and long, white clouds.

Hours later – she would one day confess that she had overdosed me on poppy and hemlock having regarded my large size and, being forced to guess at the appropriate dose, had miscalculated – I awoke to find myself stiff, sore, tightly bandaged, and arrow-free. The next two weeks or so went by in a haze of potions and salves, of sleeping draughts and bizarre dreams. When I finally surfaced, my nurse declared me cured and bobbed a curtsey to my feeble thanks. "I will reward you well," I told her, "and Count Ramon will reward you, also. Come with me to Toulouse." She needed no urging, and three days later we were riding east, her trappings on the mule and her life in the mountains now only a receding memory.

Chapter XXIII: Simon
Alaric

My father arrived in Toulouse like the warrior he is. He simply rode right through the besiegers' lines, leading a laden pack mule and followed by a dark-haired woman on a bay horse.

As calm as you like, he emerged into view of the citadel on the far side of the chaussee of the Bazacle ford, gestured airily to the troopers of de Montfort's who were stationed there, and casually rode past them at a slow pace. He moved through a maze of muddy earthworks jumbled with construction timbers, and past wooden platforms which supported catapults that were hurling large stones or arrow-headed bolts at the iron-strapped gates of the citadel. None even thought to challenge him. The two riders arrived at the line of the stone dam-cum-ford called the Bazacle, splashed through the water and emerged under our walls, where he bellowed up to the bemused watchers above: "They can't kill me. Open the postern!" And Frederick de Banastre re-entered Toulouse, citadel of the man we wanted to rule England.

I went to meet him and was shocked at his battered and bruised appearance: eyes swollen almost closed, facial wounds and splinted hands. He climbed painfully from his horse muttering about his ribs, and before he even greeted me said: "I lost the bloody sword. All that trouble and I've lost the thing!" I was puzzled. Bloodblade was at his side, as always. "Tristan's sword," he almost snarled. "The damn thing that was supposed to inspire an army."

All I could say was "How?" He looked at me with scorn.

"Bastard ambushed us. Is Gardiner here? No? Then I'm probably the only survivor. They shot us flat. You're the last of our Templars now. Is that altar of mine still safe?" I nodded.

"Safe and sound, in my chamber."

"Keep it that way," he grunted. "I'm off to talk to Ramon. We have some serious planning to do, we can't expect anything from Aragon now and Ranulf, with his own concerns in Egypt, plainly won't be coming."

Frederick was correct. Earl Ranulf was on crusade and was moreover reluctant to defy the Pope and take the side of the problematic Cathars. Better to stay away. Meanwhile, the boy king James of Aragon's advisors and regents urged caution and would not involve themselves deeper in what was an undeclared civil war in France. Before his death, Pope Innocent had turned the northern French loose on their fellow countrymen of the south, claiming it as a crusade to stamp out heresy. It was really an expedition of plunder and murder designed to strengthen Rome's hold over the whole southern part of France. The French king was offended, for the southern nobles answered to him and his holdings were being looted, but the pope overrode Louis' complaints and the crusade went forward. Shrewd Innocent had chosen a clever and determined warrior, Simon de Montfort to perform the task, and he had craftily ceded his conquests to his king, knowing he would gain enough favour to be able to keep most of them anyway.

It did not take long for de Montfort to retake the city, but he still had to take the citadel, and for that he needed a siege train. So we held out through the winter of 1217-18 and made occasional sallies to disrupt the siege works, but as summer approached, the earl constructed some heavy timber war machines to breach our defences and, under the shelter of heavy-roofed galleries, filled in the moat at several places as well as sinking a large barge at the base of the curtain wall. He had used these footholds to attempt escalades – scaling the walls with ladders, usually at several places simultaneously in hopes of finding weakened resistance to a sudden rush of fighting men, but had not been successful.

Count Ramon and I had not been idle. We had overseen the construction of timber hoards, or fighting platforms, along the length of the battlements; we had built engines of our own to hurl missiles at the siege trenches and we had reinforced our defences with the fabric of stone and timber we had taken from buildings we had pulled down inside the walls. "We need the fire breaks anyway," the count said as we watched a beautiful small chapel demolished and its stone hauled away to reinforce the walls and to be used as missiles.

But outside our walls were war engines that filled me with dread. De Montfort had dragged close to our defences not one but two vast constructs called tortoises or *cats*. They were wheeled roofs made of iron and heavy timber that could withstand the rain of rocks, boiling liquids and missiles that would pour down on them. They were even clad in uncured hides to repel fire. Inside each housing was a long, iron-tipped battering ram that swung from the apex of its steeply-pitched roof. Squads of men sheltering under the roofs swung the great ram over and over at the same point of the wall, sometimes after fires had been set alongside it to weaken the cement and loosen the stonework.

The besiegers had attempted to undermine one of our towers, but the rocky ground proved too difficult to work and that tactic failed. But day by day, the zig zag approach of the siege trenches edged closer, as miners working behind the protection of huge wicker baskets filled with soil crept towards our walls. I remarked on the slowness of their approach and Frederick, who had seen many sieges before, nodded. "Aye, they're in no rush. De Montfort has likely called on his vassals to be ready for their 40 days' annual military service, and he has probably opted to start it once we get some good weather. He can literally prepare the ground for the arrival of his reinforcements, then hurl them at us in the long days of summer."

One other engine loomed ominously near the wall, a siege tower the height of ten tall men that allowed de Montfort's archers and slingers to fire missiles down onto the fighting platforms it overtopped. We called it *Malvoisin* for 'Evil Neighbour,' and it dominated our thinking just as it dominated our wall. Four times we sallied out to attack and burn the tower, four times we were repulsed. We knew that some day those failed attacks would cost us, for once de Montfort wheeled it right up to the ramparts, he could pour men across our defences.

I had expected de Montfort to send emissaries to demand our surrender, but none came. Count Ramon explained it, sadly. "Most soldiers follow tradition and offer honourable negotiation and our surrender before they break our walls and crush our garrison. That way, they attain what they wish: the capture of the city, and they save their own and our lives.

"The old Romans established the protocol. If the garrison surrendered before the first battering ram smashed into the first gate or wall, they could walk away alive. But if the garrison forced the besiegers to begin hostilities that inevitably led to the slighting of the castle, no mercy would be offered. Simon de Montfort does not want our castle as much as he wants our blood and bones. We are heretics to be martyred. He has killed all the Cathars he could take; he is on a crusade to purge us from France."

Frederick heard the count's conclusion as he walked into the chamber. "Yes, he is, but he is reaching a crisis time. He has stripped the countryside bare and unless his masters can send considerable quantities of supplies, he'll starve himself out in a couple more months, especially if more knights arrive to do their military service."

He coughed and spat into the fire. "Anyway, good news. One of our mangonels has just crippled the tortoise they were trundling up to the Touzet rampart. We should make a sortie and burn the thing while we can."

In minutes, we were scrambling together a force of knights, men at arms, archers, axe men and labourers to carry bundles of faggots and brush, buckets of oil and other incendiaries before the enemy could ready their defences. We poured out of a sally port, knights galloping ahead to establish a perimeter, foot soldiers and the rest trotting behind. A few northern knights galloped at us but were easily repulsed, then a dozen or so swarmed out behind Guy de Montfort, Simon's younger brother, plainly identifiable by the white lion on his red shield even at the 100 paces' distance. I spurred my destrier forward and waved my good blade Hwyl, intending to confront de

Montfort myself. I was shouting 'Tailles hauts!' – 'swords up!'
to two knights who were with me when I saw de Montfort
sway violently He would have fallen from his mount if he had
not been firmly braced by his high-pommelled saddle.

A quarrel fired by one of our crossbowmen had hit him,
and a roar went up from our archers on the fighting platforms.
Two of the knight's own foot soldiers grabbed his horse's
bridle and began easing their lord down and I glanced around,
wondering if I should race across to dispatch him. Frederick
saw my indecision. "Forget him. Fire the damned tortoise!" he
yelled. "Just keep those bastards at bay!"

I looked back to where de Montfort was now on the turf.
A knight whose horse bore the same trapper – white lion on
a crimson background - who must be Count Simon himself,
was galloping to the spot, and was halting at the side of the
downed knight. Around me, a melee had developed as our
foot soldiers slaughtered the largely-unarmed men who had
been moving the tortoise. The besiegers were using baulks of
timber, iron bars and axes as clumsy defensive weapons but
were being hacked down by our soldiers. A sudden roar went
up, a roar that started on our ramparts and flowed like a tidal
wave across the killing ground.

Frederick was yelling in exultation, and pointing Bloodblade.
I followed the direction, saw not one but two knights in
identical surplices of white lion on red field. The de Montforts.

Astonishingly, both were stretched on the turf and two men at arms were kneeling alongside. Frederick's yell came to me; "They hit him with a bloody mangonel! They've flattened Simon!" Up on our parapet, small figures were dancing, waving their arms.

"They're women!" I shouted to my father.

"Aye, they're women who can operate artillery!" he called back. "They hit Simon right in the head. The bastard has to die of that!"

Stinking black smoke was choking me and my horse skittered and passaged unhappily. The tortoise was well alight, bright, grasping fingers of flame flaring up the inner walls and curling under its over-arching roof. My throat was thick with the stench of the cowhides that covered the outside of the roof, for even they were scorching and putting out dense smoke as the interior timbers caught and glowed. The enemy had no interest in us, we could no longer see the de Montforts on the turf for the crowd around them, a crowd that scattered as another large rock splashed into the mob and dispersed them like water droplets. I turned my horse and entered the city through the sally port. Inside the walls, a mob of dancing, cheering citizens and soldiery were carrying four or five women on their shoulders.

A passing archer, delirious with joy, shouted up to me: "They killed him! A few women killed de Montfort!" I leaned down to question him. "They were operating a mangonel on St James' Tower and they fired a rock that struck him right in the head as he went to help his brother," he shouted. "People saw his skull pulped!" I shook my own head. The warrior who had terrorized the Languedoc for a generation, who had rampaged in blood and fire and cruelty was no more, brought low by a handful of peasant women defending their homes with a whiplike catapult.

"They'll be laughing about that in Hell," I said aloud.

Chapter XXIV: Baziege
Frederick

Killing de Montfort changed everything. I told Alaric that the gutless bastards who'd come to plunder and rape the defenceless Cathars didn't have the balls to take over from the ambitious Simon, and anyway there was almost not a single well-placed nobleman who could be a leader of that mob even if he did screw up his courage to take on the task.

"The French poseurs will parade around in the lists preening and posing in their elaborate armour and wearing some whore's favour, but they don't want to come out in the mud and blood to face an English sword," I told him, and with some satisfaction soon learned that I was right.

The newly-installed Pope Honorius saw control of southern France and a vast fortune slipping away if Count Ramon retained his lands in the Pays d'Oc, so he pressured King Philippe to do something. Reluctantly, and very slowly, taking more than a year, the French monarch sent his son Louis to boost Simon de Montfort's 26 years old son Amaury in his efforts to defeat Count Ramon. Then, just to be safe, Philippe dithered and delayed for almost another year until the dust settled.

Ramon and I, with the Count of Foix and Alaric, who was now the last Templar of our contingent, paraded the Holy Shroud widely through the region to inspire the troops, and gathered a number of untrained followers, too. With them and our own troops, we took on a rabble of northern French knights at a place called Baziege and gave them a thrashing in a rare open battle. It was a watershed moment. While we recaptured Ramon's holdings, Amaury and Louis settled down to sieges and finally had a 'triumph' when the city of Marmande surrendered in June 1219. The duo vengefully slaughtered every human in the place, 5,000 in all, and came back to besiege the citadel of Toulouse again.

The siege did not last. Louis got cold feet and after a month returned north and the next year passed in a blur as we campaigned across the Languedoc retaking Count Ramon's possessions one after another in a steady stream. At the capture of Castelnaudary, Guy de Montfort, who had after all survived the crossbow quarrel at Toulouse, was finally killed.

By now, the count and his vassals had recaptured most of his territory, and the crusade against the Cathars had so cooled that the parfaits resurfaced and the Catholic bishops prudently fled. It was time for Alaric and I to join our seigneur Ranulf in Egypt on the Fifth Crusade, where he was besieging the port of Damietta.

Then, word also came from England, of the death of the

regent, William Marshal, the more trustworthy of the two who protected our boy king's interests. "He has been buried in our Templar church in London," Alaric informed me as he read the dispatch.

My reaction was to wonder: "Can we trust Longsword, now he is the only regent?" It might be politic for me to return to England with the Empress' crown so the northern barons could properly coronate our little king, who at age 12 might now be old enough to rule. I went to see Count Ramon.

He was cordial, for his territories were being restored; the Holy Shroud – I shuddered as he crossed himself and wondered who would shrive me of that deception - was not only a wonderful sign of the protection of God, but also had brought many to the count's forces. Also, he mused politely, although it was a pity we had lost the sword of Tristan, maybe one day he would recover it from those brigands at Pau. I nodded, speechlessly.

Soon enough, I had to speak my piece, but even when I outlined my suggestions, I did not give either the count or my own son Alaric the whole truth. Of course Alaric had no idea the Shroud was a forgery, and to them both I said merely that I would return to England to discuss with the northerners if the boy Henry of Winchester was mature enough to be king. He would be assisted by the rebel barons who were no rebels but royalists, I declared. Nor did I tell Ramon that I possessed the Holy Roman Empress' crown, or that Alaric would be guardian of England's ruby Ring of Unity that once belonged to Alfred the Great.

Lastly, we asked Ramon's blessing on Alaric's leaving to join the Fifth Crusade. "King Andrew of Hungary, Duke Leopold and the King of Jerusalem are doing God's work in Egypt," Alaric explained, although Ramon knew that perfectly well. Quite what was his opinion of God's work after Pope Innocent had set the crusader dogs onto him to carry it out, I never discovered, but being publicly stripped and flogged by covetous churchmen must have created some rancour in Ramon. However, the count was generous, Alaric was released, as was I and, with our secret treasures concealed, we said our farewells.

"You have it safe?" I asked anxiously. Alaric grinned.

"Yes, Father," he said dutifully, tapping his chest. He had the great ruby ring looped on a double chain around his neck, the gem itself snug in a leather pouch. "And you?" he raised an eyebrow. I patted the small satchel at my saddle bow. Inside was the flat lindenwood box that contained the Empress' crown. The case was lightweight enough to seem fragile but actually well-designed and highly protective. We two carried the double icons of England, and had separated them, for safety. That is how we rode out of Toulouse on our separate ways.

Alaric's journey took him across the Inland Sea to a crusade;

mine led me through the Pillars of Hercules, and to disaster.

The voyage from Marseille went well at first and we slid between Africa and Europe on a silky outflow of tide in a mist-shrouded dawn. Our vessel, which the captain had blessed by a local priest before we left Marseille, was an oak-built cog, with single-mast and square-rigging. She was built in the Baltic, was about 70 paces long and about eight paces wide in the beam; seams packed tightly with moss and her hull tarred.

Her builders had made her sturdy, with strong ribs and lapstrake planking all double-clenched with iron nails. As is the new fashion in shipbuilding, she had no open hull, but a deck above the flush-laid flat bottom that let her settle level in harbour and – an innovation – a central, stern-mounted hanging rudder which attracted much comment in port in southern France, as it was a Baltic invention not before seen there.

"She is a fine strong ship," said her master proudly. "She is no coaster but a proper seagoing workhorse." On our voyage, she carried a cargo of sweet wine and dried lavender from the Languedoc and a small but precious consignment of spices and silks that had come via Genoa from the East. I was one of only four passengers and shared a small cabin with the others, where we slept, ate and were to remain out of the crew's way if we encountered bad weather.

The captain, a swarthy Greek called Demetrio who said he

did most of his trading in the Baltic, generally carried wine to England, collected cloth and wool for delivery to the Baltic and exchanged it for a cargo of amber, furs and hides for his return journey to the Mediterranean.

"This is a good time of year to sail," he said, "although the Gulf of Gascony, which the Spanish call Viscaya and you English say is Biscay, is a dangerous place. We have two main choices. The swifter route is to go far out into the Atlantic where the water is deep and the swells are even, but you will be very far from land if there is trouble or the weather worsens, and it is difficult to find your way even at the best of times.

"The alternative is to stay close to the coast, a longer, slower route but generally safer. There is though, the threat of being trapped by the west wind so you cannot round Monte Facho, the headland of Fisterra, or the wind may drive your ship into the rocky maze of islands off Ouessant, in Brittany, where there are frequent sea fogs.

"You should only sail the coastal route when the weather is good, because the water of the bay gets suddenly shallow. If the wind rises, the big ocean waves from the west pile up and steepen on the shallows. They are very big when they slam into the shore, and then wash back out. It creates a maelstrom of murderous fast tide rips from all directions that will swamp your vessel. So, if you are inside the bay and even a small storm blows up, you have to run fast for shelter. If you delay, you will be unable to get into port through those tides and you will not be able to escape from the sharp fangs of the coast because you cannot sail west, into the wind that will inevitably push you onto those fangs."

The information made me suck my own teeth. "So we will take the ocean route?" I asked.

Demetrio flashed his big smile. "No, we take the coast. I have to stop in Bayona and Santander. If the weather is bad, we will just sit in the port and drink wine until it improves. It will be a pleasant voyage."

The ocean god Manannan mac Lir must have howled laughing. The Christ might have been able to walk on water but nothing could have strolled across the seas Manannan sent that next week.

We had been blown along like thistledown and were well north along the coast of Portugal when something roused me from my sleep. I went on deck in the wolf light that comes before the dawn to see a yellow cast to the sky. The underlying swells of the Atlantic seemed disturbed, irregular. I looked for Demetrio but he was not at the stern. In the captain's usual place was a phlegmatic sailor whose name I never knew. He muttered sullenly when I asked about Demetrio. "Sleeping, we had trouble during the night." He spat over the side. I considered his insolence but decided to wait until we were ashore before I punished him, so went back to my paillasse and fell into a broken sleep.

It was full daylight when I awoke and the ship's motion was disturbing. Out on deck, the wind was whistling, sending long white streamers of foam in parallel lines across the crumbling wave crests, which were half-obscured in flying mist. We were jolting from crest to trough, thumping down hard, then swooping sickeningly upwards. Demetrio, half-dressed and wild-haired, seemed to have only just arrived on deck, he was cursing and shouting orders to the handful of crew. The vessel came around sluggishly to head in the direction I assumed was the shore. Almost at once there was a loud cracking jolt, a splintering noise and the ship flew sideways. The rudder, centrally mounted at the stern and novelty object of such interest among the southern sailors before we left Marseille, had torn completely away.

The crew were working frantically to haul in the sail, Demetrio was dragging a large piece of canvas from its storage and we were rocking sideways like a child's cradle, almost dipping each gunwale alternately under the hissing green waves. "Get this over the side, make a sea anchor," Demetrio yelled, busily lashing a length of rope to a corner of the canvas.

Alarmed shouting came from the ship's bow. A sailor had fallen overside. As we both turned, I saw three of his comrades run to the rail. Demetrio recognised the danger before they did and screamed an urgent warning, but it was too late. A steep-sided pyramid of grey-green ocean was looming over the bow, swamping it then smashing down in a fury of white water. We saw it and just had time. It engulfed us chest-deep as we clung desperately to the stanchions that had supported the rudder.

My feet left the deck, but I maintained a death-grip and the killing torrent subsided. The sailors at the rail had vanished. The ship was skidding sideways before the wind, her flat bottom allowing little purchase on the water and she was tilted alarmingly. Apart from Demetrio, I could see no crewmen. "Axe, get an axe!" the captain was screaming at me as he staggered up the slanting deck. He pulled out his sheath knife and began sawing at a thick hempen rope. I glanced upwards and saw that the rope was a support for the creaking mast, whose wind-thrusted leverage was forcing one rail almost under water.

I stumbled across the pitch of the deck to the small sleeping cabin where my travelling companions were clutching at any supports they could. My big sword Bloodblade was tucked under my paillasse, I grabbed him and staggered back up the steepening deck boards to begin hacking at the mast's restraining ropes. One broke almost instantly, lashing viciously past my face. I was more cautious with the others, but they separated safely enough under Bloodblade's keen edge until there was just one heavy length of cordage left.

I hacked at it, Demetrio sawed with his knife, then he swore and jerked back. Water squeezed from the rope spurted as the fibres tensioned under the sway and pull of the ship and the last few uncut strands snapped. The heavy cable whipped free, catching Demetrio across the temple and dropping him cold. He began to slide down the planking and I lunged to grab him but a wall of green wave smashed into me as it raced down the length of the ship. I was swept with it, banging my knee into something before I was carried hard into a rudder stanchion. The big roller's power wrapped me around the upright, bending me like a horse's shoe and drove every bit of breath from my lungs. I sucked in salt water, felt my head bang against something, surfaced for a second or several, vomited water and was engulfed again.

As I came into air, I spewed out more saltwater and gulped oxygen down my burning throat. I had my body and arms wrapped around the stanchion for safety, but the ship seemed more level, though the wind was still howling wildly and lines of spindrift flew like cotton through the air. I heard a dull thumping from the ship's side and saw the cause: the snapped-off mast was still tethered by the cordage we had not cut, and the hefty pine trunk that had held up our sail was now a steadying sea anchor, although it was a dangerous one that was both saving us from swamping and at the moment was also trying to stave in the hull of our ship.

Better cut those ropes, too, Freddy, I told myself and even in my own mind I heard the slurred tone and knew I was less than at my best. Bloodblade was lying where he had been washed, into the scuppers, and I retrieved him then stumbled on the tossing deck to open the sleeping cabin door. One man remained inside, a plump Frankish wool merchant. No other person was in sight along the deck. "Where is everyone?" I asked him in Occitan, then tried again in Germanic.

He rolled his eyes at me, plainly terrified. "The other two they went and not return."

"Come and help," I demanded. "We have to cut this away from the ship." He eyed Bloodblade uncertainly. Was I threatening to kill him?

"I have silver," he said, but he made no move away from his bunk. I shrugged, waved and moved to do the work myself. It took an age of hacking and slashing while the turbulent ocean threatened at any moment to wash me overboard, but I lashed myself to the ruined rail and survived two huge waves that threw me sideways. Finally, the last cord was cut and the menacing battering ram that had been our mast pitched and rolled away.

The ship was low in the water, rolling sluggishly now, and it was easier to move about. I drank thirstily from the stoppered jug of water that was lashed near the tiller and explored the ship. Not one other person aboard. On an impulse, I moved among the huge wooden tuns that contained wine and knocked the bungs out of them with the butt of my knife. When they had emptied, I thought I'd hammer the stoppers back in again, maybe that would help keep the ship buoyant.

I could not tell in which direction we were moving, but the wind was propelling the hulk briskly enough and there was nothing I could do, so I gathered one of my saddlebags and, shivering, pushed a cloak and some gold into it, then tied to my belt the small saddlebow bag which contained the cased crown. I looked at Bloodblade with regret. The only way I could keep him was if we were driven ashore. I would not wear him as I swam and I could not carry him. I hoped we would simply go ashore. I stabbed him deep into the decking. At least he would not go alone to the bottom of the ocean.

The plump merchant was weaving out of the little cabin. "Where is the land?" he asked.

"Just over there," I said, encouragingly. "It's not far."

But it was.

The storm continued unrelenting and the merchant died two nights later. I would have joined him except for the water jug that I refilled with wine and for the heavy cloak I wrapped around my shaking self. The blasting wind never really abated, and I had no idea where it was hurling me although sometimes to my right hand I had glimpses of a long grey coastline with headlands and white breakers at the foot of steep, forbidding cliffs. We never seemed to get closer to the shore, and I deduced that the rollers that crashed against them surged back to keep my increasingly-battered vessel at a distance.

Amazingly, although the hull was half filled with saltwater, the emptied wine tuns I had re-bunged provided enough buoyancy to keep the mastless hulk afloat. My concern was that the battering of the semi-buoyant tuns inside the hull was causing the decking to lift. In time the ship would simply shake itself to pieces. For myself, I was weakening. It looked like it would be a race: would the ship founder before I did? My lips were cracked and bleeding, my eyes were swollen near-shut, I had salt sores and cuts, sprains and bruises everywhere. My right ribs, which had almost healed from the arrow strike, had been battered again when I crashed into a stanchion and the sharp pain when I coughed or even breathed deeply suggested I had re-broken the things.

That day, to my right, I saw distant plumes of spray and heard the boom of the big Atlantic rollers on rocks. I was perilously close to a shore I knew must be rocky, dangerous, and likely fatal to me and the ship. Later in the day, the light brightened, the clouds thinned and behind me I saw a gleam of sun. I decided that I was being driven east, racing towards what I did not know. The wind veered – I could tell that now that I had a notion of direction – and it was coming from the west and north. From what I recalled from the Greek master's descriptions of the coast, I had probably rounded the two main headlands of the voyage, but I was being driven deep into the grim embrace of another west-facing bay.

I clutched for my neck amulet of Thor, the small silver hammer *mjollnir* that had for so long protected my life. "I never was a good Christian even though I went on crusade against the Saracens. I went to Acre to fight for Richard," I told whichever god was listening. "Well, I have never consciously been evil, I've only lived my life as a soldier and sometimes you do things that are cruel." It was as close as I could come to shriving my soul, and I just hoped that the Christ god would not take amiss my forging his burial shroud.

"That was just to help raise an army against an unjust invader," I explained, but the only recipient of my confession seemed to be a wind-blown petrel that scudded by on storm-driven wings.

The watery sun faded and, wrapped in my cloak and jammed between the life-saving stanchions, I slipped into a doze. How long I slept I have no way of telling, but I awoke to a violent motion of the ship, which was bucking like an unbroken horse. I seemed to be in a fast-racing river of whitened foam that curved and swirled. There was some daylight, and it showed edges of white along the fogged horizon that surrounded me. I was stupid with weakness but gradually it dawned on me that I was being swept across the flats of a wide and shallow bay.

I was being carried in my flat-bottomed hulk on an incoming tide that sought and followed the riverine gullies it had carved in the sand and went at the pace of a cantering horse.

A cog with a deeper hull would have grounded, broken up and thrown me out to drown. This trader's vessel, designed to creep into the shallows of rivers and coastal inlets, drew so little water it was carrying me like a chariot over the bed of a wide bay. Ahead of me, looming out of the fog, was a huge dark shadow, its base limned in white surf. It was a sea mount, a sea-girt citadel set in the middle of a bay and I was being washed towards it by a combination of racing tide and raging wind. This, Freddy my boy, is your chance, I muttered. I threw off my cloak in case it hampered me, checked the leather bag with its precious contents that was fixed to my belt and inched my way forward to the bow of the scudding hulk.

Then I went back and retrieved Bloodblade. If I was going to drown, I wanted to die sword in hand.

I had not quite re-reached the bow when the ship struck and I was thrown forward, slamming my head against the upper strake of planking before I went over the side into the foaming water. What happened next is unclear but I found myself on hands and knees, still clutching Bloodblade, in a surge of seawater only a couple of feet deep. Behind me, the hulk had broached, foundered on the sandbank where I was crouched and was now heeled on its side, happily providing me with some protection from the force of the racing tide which flooded by on each side. I lurched upright and painfully pushed through the swirling water and sucking sand to move higher up the small islet, where a clump of sea grasses told me I had a chance to remain just barely above the water level.

And there I sat, Bloodblade driven deep like a stake into the sand between my feet, my hands grasping his hilt in case a wave swept over me. I was shaking with cold and also with relief. A long hour later, a fishing boat came out of the mist. Someone had seen the hulk's wild career across the tide and had come to investigate. I was saved. My size and sword kept the fishermen respectful, or they might have followed the time honoured practice of wreckers along the coast and finished me off, but I waved them to the hulk and told them: "It's all yours. Keep the wine. There should be spices there, too."

At my quiet demand, one of the villains retrieved my saddlebag from the sleeping cabin and I gave him gold. Then they rowed me to the citadel on the sea mount which they told me the Romans built and called Mons Tomba, but the good monks whose priory held the crest now called Mont Saint Michele. I didn't care. I just wanted a bed and sleep, but first I had to speak with the slab-faced gate guard captain and answer his questions, then I faced an interminable number of steps up the steep sides of the mount before I wearily reached the dormitory where I would be sheltered.

An old nun and a young monk showed me to a chamber where the youth brought me food and a bowl of hot, thin soup while the nun bound up a gash in my scalp and a few others of my obvious wounds. I was just taking my second draught of soup when the door opened and a younger nun came in, bowing. "This, Lord Frederick," she said, "is Abbess Frances," and Blanche, my Blanche, stepped lightly into the room.

She smiled at me. "They told me you were here."

I must have been staring at her, foggily uncomprehending, but I managed to rally, "I have a great deal to tell you."

Blanche smiled again, and said softly: "And I greatly wish to hear it."

Historical Notes

This narrative has stayed as true as possible to the chronology of events from the time of Magna Carta (1215 AD) to the capture of Damietta by the forces of the Fifth Crusade (1219 AD). Many characters are taken straight from the pages of history and are presented as accurately as possible.

King John, for example, popularly known as Robin Hood's enemy, generally deserves the terrible reputation history has given him. He was treacherous, tyrannical, venal, and a serial sexual predator. He was an efficient administrator but like his brother Richard Lionheart, regarded England only as an income stream for his other interests, which lay in France.

A coalition of barons tired of being bled white by his many and inventive taxes forced his hand with Magna Carta but their concern was less noble than the emancipation of the common people. It was simply to curb the king, make him answerable to the law and ease their own ruinous tax burdens. The charter basically spelled out how they could legally oppose their sworn lord if he failed to live up to its strictures.

Our hero Frederick was entangled in all this: his liege lord was Ranulf of Chester, who was John's man, but Frederick sympathized with the rebel English barons of the north and was reluctant to act either for or against Ranulf.

Our story says Frederick took his opportunity when John's baggage train was swamped and even today, researchers dispute not only where the royal treasure might be, but if it even went down with the wagons at all. A hoarder of jewels, it is not unlikely that John kept his valuables close, and he certainly took the longer, safer route around the Wash and avoided the disaster. The question is: were the jewels and regalia with him?

Positing that he was planning to pawn them to fund his military activities has merits: nobles pawned their valuables as an accepted practice of the day. It was John's misfortune that he was taken ill and died soon after the disaster and ours in that it leaves a mystery about the treasure.

The monk Walter who helped hide the stolen regalia came from Pinchbeck, a place close to Swineshead Abbey where John stayed after the disaster at the Wash, and he went on to become abbot of Chester, where Frederick's overlord Ranulf ruled. It is possible to speculate that Walter, being in the right places at the correct times, was in fact linked to the missing treasure and Frederick's seigneur.

The monks of Stanlaw (now called Stanlow) did evacuate their abbey by the Mersey after it was flooded several times. They relocated to build another abbey at Whalley, in the demesne of the Banastres, whose Norman manor house Bank Hall was rebuilt in the 1500s and survived in one form or another until the second world war, when it was used as a military establishment. A recent renovation has restored the site at Bretherton, Lancashire, and the Bannister armorial bearings, earned at a tournament at Stamford in the 14th century, are still displayed in Whalley Abbey's stained glass to this day. More on the abbey window in the next book...

Much of the narrative is concerned with having the proper regalia for a legitimate coronation. This was a vital need of the day, as the throne had numbers of claimants, and only those who could demonstrate their legitimacy by bloodline, conquest or other persuasion could expect an uncontested crowning or settled reign. It was why kings were so eager to have male heirs whose rights could not be challenged, and why at one stage of the narrative three children of age 12 or less occupied thrones in England, Spain and Aragon. King John's son Henry III – the numbering convention is a more modern invention, so his contemporaries knew him as Henry of Winchester – was only nine years old when he succeeded to the throne and after his hasty coronation at Gloucester it was considered wise to hold a second, confirmatory crowning four years later at Westminster.

So, the traditions and regalia were important (and the Empress Matilda's crown really was made to fold flat for transportation). Which leads to the other icons, the ruby ring which reputedly once belonged to Alfred the Great (and would become property of the Black Prince and later still of England's current monarch); the Sword of Tristan – vanished with John's other baubles – and the faked Holy Shroud commissioned by Frederick.

The wily old soldier knew the value of religious icons, which were deeply ingrained in the culture of the age, and to have the protection of the Shroud wrapped around the spirit of his army was a powerful and inspirational shield. Whether the Turin shroud is a fake like Frederick's, we may never know, but there are similarities and the Turin shroud was looted from the Boucoleon palace in Constantinople, the same source Frederick claimed for his manufactured grave raiment.

Frederick of course had the idea of an inspirational icon but he did not understand that some people more spiritual than he actually were in touch with psychic abilities or intuitions. There's an example in his conversation with St Denys, who foresaw that six centuries later, when Longsword's tomb at Salisbury was opened in 1791, a dead rat containing traces of arsenic poison would indeed be found inside the Crusader's skull. The creature is now on display at the Salisbury and Wilts Museum.

St Denys also casually spoke of the Stonehenge blue stones as moved by water and music. Recent research indicates that the stones were formed naturally as columns four or more

millions of years ago. They were split by quarrymen from
their rock face just as ice does the same damage in nature.
The canny ancients knew that a wooden wedge, driven into
a outcrop's cracks then watered, would swell and split the
rock for them. What St Denys intuited was what 21st century
researchers are positing: that the smaller bluestone monoliths
were first used to form another memorial elsewhere – likely in
Wales – a half-millennium before they were transported with
great labour to Salisbury Plain. Legend spoke of the great
rocks being moved by music and water, which translates as
rhythmic chanting of those who hauled the slabs, which they
likely moved on sledges and timber rails and floated on rivers.
(The larger sarsen stones were quarried locally).

The power of older beliefs over Christianity is also
demonstrated in the matter of Tristan's sword. Frederick and
the rebel barons wanted to install Raymond VI / Ramon of
Toulouse as a reliable regent. Handing over a token of the
English regalia would have been powerful evidence of the
commitment of the rebel barons to his cause – even if it was
a fake weapon, which Ramon must not suspect. Alaric was
less sure of its provenance, which was why Frederick did not
let Alaric accompany him on his journey to Spain: father and
son had been estranged for so long they hardly knew each
other and Frederick felt Alaric was too straight an arrow to
countenance any *ruse de guerre*.

*

Cathars

The horrors of Pope Innocent's crusade to exterminate the austerely pious Cathars are not exaggerated. Half a million people were slaughtered – sometimes whole cities emptied, like Beziers, where 7,000 were killed. Simon de Montfort (not to be confused with his eponymous son the rebel earl of Leicester, who 750 years ago established the foundations of England's parliament) led the Albigensian Crusade and waged a fearsome war of terror against the 'heretics.' Unfortunate Cathars were burned, hanged, mutilated , blinded, used for target practice or dragged to their deaths behind horses. Even the dead were exhumed to be burned. It was all to strengthen Rome's grip on southern France and the regional ruler, Count Ramon of Toulouse, who refused the order to wage war on his own people was not exempt from humiliation, loss and suffering.

De Montfort died as the narrative tells it – struck by a stone from a catapult fired by several women during the siege of Toulouse. The new pope had no replacement for his zealot warlord and Ramon spent some months re-taking his possessions from the disjointed northern French, hearing tales of the crusaders' fury that would be hard to exaggerate.

Nor are the reports exaggerated of the secretiveness and fanaticism of the brotherhood of the Templars, who themselves later underwent what Ramon suffered. The militant friars were first onto the battlefield, last off it and were rightly feared for their fighting skills, monastic obedience, discipline and devotion.

At the other end of the religious scale, ordinary monks ignored the tenets of St Benedict to live plainly, and indulged themselves, often luxuriously. Monks from the cathedral at Durham, for example, had servant-tended holidays of several weeks at a time at their own recreation centre on the River Wear at nearby Finchale Priory. Stories abounded about Finchale's population of ageing prostitutes and laymen made jokes about the well-worn whores of Wear getting big indulgences.

Many monks had secret wives, but their more usual indulgence was gluttony. Record rolls show that at large abbeys like that of Westminster, a cleric engaged in non-physical pursuits would normally consume more than 4,000 calories per day, or twice what a field labourer ate, and the monks were ingenious at evading the rules of meatless fasting, often not fasting at all. Many chose to interpret the church's strictures as applying only to meals taken in the refectory, and simply ate elsewhere in the abbey.

Of course, the nobility feasted too. For them, a meal was both a mark of status and an opportunity to eat the most exotic food they could. Taste was less important than rarity; variety and the most elaborate foods were vital to their standing. Peacock, swan and heron were typical wildfowl dishes; the everyday was carp, pike and other fish, all raised in special ponds and were a regular part of their diet, as was venison, pork and salted meats. They had interesting beliefs about the different digestive systems of rich and poor and held that there was a natural link between a person's work and his diet: rough labourers, they believed, needed coarser, cheaper food; noblemen ate more refined dishes which they flavoured with exotic spices to sustain their more refined bodies.

Finally, the account of Frederick's voyage outlines the dilemma faced by those bold sailors of square-rigged vessels. Unable to sail against the wind, if they wished to cross Biscay they had the option of leaving land far behind and trusting themselves to the great Atlantic and its smooth but vast rollers to help them cross the dangers of the continental shelf, or they could follow the coast and risk a sudden storm that could pile up the ocean against the stumbling block of the shelf. Even if they succeeded, they could still find themselves trapped, driven by the wind and unable to round the headlands of Finisterre or Ushant. And even if they managed that, they still faced the treacherous rocks and shoals of Brittany…

Acknowledgements

This third book of the 'Crusader' series follows my six-book 'Forgotten Emperor' series and shifts the scene from Roman Britain to the early medieval period. On the face of it, turning out just another book should be a mechanical matter, a thing done by rote, but that was not the case.

Without the support, input, encouragement, ideas and assistance of my wife Jennie, it is unlikely even one book would be finished by now and I would be a despairing wreck babbling and crooning to myself in a dark corner. So, my first nod and deepest gratitude go to She of the Sounding Board for her patience and level-headed critiques.

A handful of others who must remain nameless also deserve gratitude for appearing as matrices for certain of the series' characters. You know who you are, Berlage, Claresta, Jacquin, Rakul et alia.

The professionals at Endeavour Press, London, have carried these books forward smoothly and efficiently, so special kudos in particular to partner Richard Foreman, publishing director Amy Durant and publisher Jack Butler. My fulsome thanks go to them, as always.

A final bow must go to US Military Academy graduate and

historian Norman 'Skip' Folden (USAF ret'd) whose insightful review of my work has inspired me to try harder and hopefully do better. Thank you, Skip. Keep firing!

Paul Bannister
Oregon 2016

About the author and his books:

Deep-rooted Lancastrian Paul Bannister was a national newspaper journalist in both the UK and USA who turned to historical fiction after researching the story of the first emperor of Britain. This was the Roman admiral Carausius, who usurped the throne for seven years (286 – 293 AD) until his death.

Carausius may be the historical source of the King Arthur legends, a theory Bannister expands in the 'Forgotten Emperor' series. ('Arthur Britannicus,' 'Arthur Imperator,' 'Arthur Invictus,' 'The King's Cavalry,' 'A Fragile Peace' and 'Arthur: War's End'). These publications are available through Amazon as e-books or in print.

The Emperor series is followed by the ongoing series: 'Crusader,' 'Treason' and now, 'Templar.' (2016)

Bannister also authored the autobiography: 'Tabloid Man and the Baffling Chair of Death; (2010) and several books on parapsychology. He lives in Oregon with his wife Jennie, a large Catahoula hound called Axel and a 21 lbs Maine Coon cat who answers to Barney at meal times.

As for his Lancastrian roots, county records show the Banastres in Bank Hall, Bretherton, in 1116 AD, a half-century after the Conquest gave them land grants there and in North Wales. The Norman Banastres were driven out of their Prestatyn motte-and-bailey stronghold by the Welsh after a century, but the author is happy to report that his cousins Eveline, Josephine, Kathleen and Ollier, Groves and Maxwell all now live within a bowshot or two of that old fortress. Perhaps they have ambitions to re-take it, 900 years later.